IN WATERMELON SALT

BOOKS BY B. ELWIN SHERMAN

The Miradors – Descensions Of A Man

George W. Bush – On The Trips Of His Tongue – A Linguistic Legacy

HumorUs (With the NetWits)

Toolkit In Paradise – The Self-Helpless Guide
To A Decade Of American Wit & Wisdom

Caught In The Shower Without A Pencil

Opening Closures – A Young Mother's Dying Declarations

Walk Tall And Carry A Big Watering Can (2011)

POETRY

The Night Dorothy Parker Begged For It

IN WATERMELON SALT

SALT

The Lost Richard Brautigan

**Dark-Humored Historic Fiction
Of Novel Proportions**

B. Elwin Sherman

Curry Burn Press ψ New Hampshire

ISBN-13: 978-0-6153829-6-8
ISBN-10: 0-6153829-6-7

First Edition, First Printing

Designed & composed in Cambria Regular at Curry Burn Press

Front cover designed by B. Elwin Sherman

Back cover photo dedicated to Judith,
taken by an unknown passing beachcomber.

Printed in the U.S.A.

Published by:
Curry Burn Press, P.O. Box 360, Bethlehem, NH 03574
www.toolkitinparadise.com

"I want something to do."

"Go nurse the soldiers," said my young neighbor, Tom, panting for "the tented field."

"I will!"

So far, very good.

Louisa May Alcott ~ Hospital Sketches

DEDICATION:

For:

Richard Gary Brautigan

Died:
2010 in Cross Corners, New Hampshire, age 75.

Date of death:
Uncertain. Sometime in late winter.

Reason for uncertainty:
Body not found until early summer.

Reason body not found until early summer: Metaphorical.

Reason for metaphor:
In Watermelon Salt

IN WATERMELON SALT

LOST BALLOON PREFACE
TO A THEATRICAL INTRODUCTION

I gave away IN WATERMELON SALT the way I would have designed it: quite by chance, when I was on my way to get something else.

Secretly, (more on that later) I surrendered these stories to a North Country antique barn called "The Fifty-Acre Wood," its name an act of open rebellion by its owner, Mrs. Martinez. She was a big fan of A.A. Milne and her husband Dale was not, so she made a bitter compromise by reducing Winnie-The-Pooh's fictional haunt to a nonfictional 50 acres. This had only served to further estrange Dale Martinez, as if his hopscotch name hadn't already done that all his life, and he'd taunted her unmercifully over it until the day he died in a terrible chainsaw accident.

Dale Martinez was a self-taught woodsman, and he forgot the lesson he'd never learned about the dangers of cutting down a tree when it was leaning into another tree. The sidewinder tree had paid attention in class, however, and had artfully done its job, dispatching him with one dull slice.

Mrs. Martinez, for her part, named it "Hooray For Isaac Newton" Day.

Foresters in these parts would agree that the number of trees per acre on the Martinez property averaged 284. Thus,

$$284 \text{ trees per acre}$$
$$14{,}200 \text{ trees in } 50 \text{ acres}$$
$$\text{Minus one tree} = 49.996\%$$

Strictly speaking, Mr. Martinez's act reduced his wife's business to the 49.996 Percent Left Standing Acre Wood, if you want to quibble over it.

I don't.

She didn't rename the business.

I did.

And I rounded it off in the same spirit that the sidewinder tree had rounded off Dale Martinez.

She did, however, have him cremated against his wishes. Then, against what legacy and dignity he ever would have imagined gaining and losing, she dumped his ashes in a rusty milk can that she kept behind the counter at the former Fifty-Acre Wood. She smoked twenty non-filtered cigarettes a day and flicked her ashes in with his, calculating that by the time she'd filled the can with her spent cigarettes she'd be dead, and no one could ever separate her butts from the hushed dumb dust of Dale Martinez.

Occasionally, when she caught herself looking at the milk can for too long, she gave it a good kick.

Vengeance, it seems, can reach into eternity and keep on going.

Her name was really Mrs. Martini, but I called her Mrs. Martinez because she looked more Spanish than Italian, and my brain could never reconcile her face with Martini. I could never say it without a "shaken, not stirred" joke dying to be unleashed. She always corrected me, and I always apologized.

"Morning, Mrs. Martinez," I said, on this particular morning.

"It's MARTINI. MAR...TIN...I! Will you NEVER get that?" she said, more than a little irritated.

More than a little irritated was her usual demeanor.

"I apologize. Mrs. MAR...TIN...I," I said, with Ian Fleming jabbing me in the ribs. I don't know how she stayed solvent in the antique business, because she treated all her customers like this, even the ones who granted her an Italian visage and got her name right, like the tourist fellow ahead of me at the counter:

"No, I don't deal with 'em. I can't give that crap away," she snapped at him. The man had asked her if she carried any 78 rpm records. He was looking for the rare French Pathé recordings with center-starts.

He'd told her: "You placed the needle on the inside of the record to begin. This reduced end-groove distortion in the music of that age, where crescendos were common. They stopped making them in the 1920's."

She'd yawned and hadn't looked up. He'd tried to explain his quest to her in detail, as people with a passion for odds-and-ends are wont to do, even with reluctant listeners who wouldn't know your odd from your end, nor care about either.

"The real speed actually varied from eighty to a hundred twenty rpm," he'd pressed on, desperate to make her enthusiastic about his enthusiasm. "So, the 'seventy-eight' part really is a misnomer." Big mistake. If the real speed rpm variable had been two million when played backwards in a lost Incan sub-dialect on wax paper, she wouldn't have been any more unimpressed.

Still, he could not let it go, and pressed further: "When they were first made, in---"

And, right there is where she knocked him out of his groove with her crap remark, halting his useless entreaty. He turned and left abruptly, grabbing his wife by the arm and leading her out. "Stupidest name for an antique shop I ever heard," he muttered. His wife didn't react. She looked like a woman whose reacting days were over.

That's when I told Mrs. MARTINI, if you please, of my search, and she directed me "back there, up and in," pointing without looking with a twist-jab-sweeping motion at the narrow aisle behind me, as if a three-tiered hand signal could convey all that.

Impossibly, it could have, I thought, and it did, without the verbal cuing. I followed the impossible gesture back there, up a winding staircase and into a small room.

By God she was right.

A locked, glass-lid consignment case displayed the item I'd been looking for: an original National Geographic Explorer II Balloon bookmark.

On November 11, 1935, two U.S. Army captains flew themselves and a balloon to a then world record altitude of 72,395 feet. They'd done it wearing football helmets and eating homemade sandwiches, a decidedly less sophisticated feat than would be attempted today.

Too bad. I prefer that vintage kind of damn the full seat-of-the-pants speed ahead torpedoes madman bravado. That tohellingone fatalistic flair of yesteryear's madcaps. All or nothing. Today's daredevils have too many Plan B's. Boring.

The National Geographic Society, knowing a good exploit when they saw one, later had the rubberized, long-staple cotton fabric of the balloon that carried the intrepid pilots cut into bookmark-sized mementos. No one knows how many were made.

I like that in my relics. Some degree of speculation keeps me interested, even if I know that it's boast and bunk.

Always the conspiracy theorist, I know why the real number was never made public: Someone could have then sized and totaled them up and determined that there were more balloon fabric souvenirs produced than there ever was balloon fabric. Not good. So, the solution was simple:

Lie.

The consignor had placed a seventy-five dollar price tag on the bookmark. In 1935, they were given free to National Geographic Society members. Add three-quarters of a century to a memento of long-gone crazy courage, and that mark-up seemed about right to me.

I was about to go out, down, and across to get Mrs. Martini-Tinez, (There. That's settled. I can only take so much equivocation. You too, no doubt.) because I needed her to come back over, up and in with me to unlock the case. That's when I noticed a box beside the table.

On the outside of it, hand-lettered:

OLD AMERICAN RIFLEMAN MAGAZINES
$20.00

The words looked like they'd been written with a dying hand. Of course, everything ever written was written with a dying hand, if you want to get philosophical about it.

I don't. Not just yet.

The letters had been hastily scribbled, and looked like they'd been done with a hand capable of going in three different directions at once. I couldn't have designed a better coffin for a writing life.

Inside the box, inside the magazines between their alternate pages, I secretly placed my original manuscript of (here we are, as promised) what you'll find in this book.

Why was I carrying it around? You're on your own with that one.

I also left there with my fragment of corrupted vintage balloon flesh. All the rest is aeronautical literature.

From here on over, up and out, you'll have to bring your own helmets and lunchboxes, and you're free to assume that the scrap of balloon fabric from the 49.996 Percent Standing Acre Wood is genuine.

I'll believe it if you will.

A RAILSPLITTER'S EPILOGUE
TO A LOST BALLOON

One more point:

Before I left the antique barn with my scandalous balloon bookmark, I asked Mrs. Martini-Tinez if she knew the provenance for it.

A dangerous move in this neck of the woods, because antique barn owners -- especially those whose woodsy neck has been reduced by .004 percent, and who drop Lucky Strikes into their husbands' eternal dustbins just for the sweet retribution of it -- are notorious tale spinners.

They'll size you up quickly, and know before you open your mouth just how much dressed-up hooey you'll accept as the truth, and perhaps the finer distinction -- how much truth you already know.

To them, that's not just a fine distinction; it's THE distinction: the bottom line of the wangler's art.

For Mrs. Martini-Tinez, it was as simple as watching how a customer first picked up and handled an item. Amateur treasure hunters were too gingerly or too rough with it. Professionals pretended to be neither.

The rookie browsers didn't stand a chance against her. She'd watch them hold and gaze at her junktiques in the light, turning the old glassware this way and that, or fanning out the ephemera and dusting off the undust-able, feigning irritation. To her, they always acted like your well-intentioned armchair dentist friends act when they attempt to diagnose your infected gums:

"Ooooh. Aaaaaah. Yeeeee. Ummmm. Yep. Looks infected."

And, in the end, it didn't matter how many vowels or consonants they haggled; she'd get her price. Sorry, dearies. A 150-year old thing should have some degree of dust & grime on it, and she knew all the degrees.

Bear with me. She's about to get her comeuppance.

Whether they entered as high-toned New York boutique dealers who'd dicker with her until they had her right where she wanted them, or they breezed in as lowbrow tourists -- the "sawbuck flatlanders" who'd always offer her an uncontested ten dollars for anything "vintage" or "antique" or even a dented rusty milk can/ashtray combo -- Mrs. Martini-Tinez had everyone's number.

Her favorite scheming business pleasure, other than the daily avenging ashflicks into Dale's milk can/urn, came after she'd made a trip to the city for a day of upscale avenue dump-picking. She'd bring the sidewalk treasures home and later sell all the castoff trash back to the same unwitting urban prigs who'd discarded it. They never caught on, and she decided that it was because they didn't want to.

Self-deception and counterfeit swank are joined at the hip.

Other signs, too, did not go unnoticed. She watched to see if their cars matched their clothes, or if their body language contradicted their spoken language. Boast and bunk were her raison d'être, and she knew what it meant when people acted this way or that. More importantly, she knew what it meant when they didn't.

She'd put a fifty dollar tag on something she wanted ten dollars for. Then:

"Would you take twenty-five for this?

"No."

"Thirty-five?

"Well, if I have to."

Or, for the same item, sometimes she'd deliberately not price it. Then:

"This isn't marked. What are you asking?"

"Hmmm. I'm not sure about that; it came from a Vermont estate sale. The heirs had been cut out because of an old family feud, and the courts found in favor of the old granny. Then, she sold everything outright just to spite the inheritors. I haven't had a chance to look that item up yet. I know I've never seen another one exactly like it. What could you offer for it?"

"Fifty dollars?"

"Well … if I have to."

As a general rule in antiquing, if the customers believe it came from an old contested Vermont estate, they're hooked.

If they also can be convinced that there is some ugly country family anecdotal tantrum chemistry tied to it -- like a wronged, embittered eccentric widow or a miserly, avenging widower and at least a hint of thievery -- they're lined and sinkered.

But, she also knew, when dealing with customers like me, (comeuppance right around the corner) that no one can know everything about everything, and most importantly, she knew that I knew she knew it, which was probably the real reason she was always especially rude to me, and not because my mind's need for Queen Isabella always trumped my mouth's want for Anna Magnani whenever I spoke her name.

When it comes to antiquities, a person can know something about everything, and everything or nothing about something, but it's impossible to know all there is to know about all that was once new, and now is old.

It's a buyer's credo that Abraham Lincoln would've reworked into a speech and armed himself with at any antique barn around here.

I knew that Mrs. Martini-Tinez didn't know who I was, or better yet who I'd been. I doubt that she could even tell you much about who she thought I wasn't.

That's why it was perfect that she become the unwitting gatekeeper of my last works.

I thought about the fate of my stories and poems, about who might one day lug home the box of old gun magazines. I wondered if they'd understand when my handwritten pages fluttered out of them.

I wished I could be there when, in between the articles on chronoscopes and powder smoke and reloading benches, they also found my tribute to a sexpot Australian bagpiper.

I wondered if they'd feel annoyed or mystified when my ode to Truman Capote as a hostile witness dropped out of the article pages that told every 1949 American Rifleman all there was to know about laminated stock blanks and the Neuhausen 47/8 pistol.

"Looks like there's no such thing as an unloaded magazine," I hoped they'd quip.

As legacies go, that would be enough for any humorist, but it didn't matter. I'd made copies. That's how you're here.

Some people, and Mrs. Martini-Tinez had been in that some-people group all her life, always cut off their noses to spite their faces. And, let's never forget that too many times in this life, the consequences of knowing or not knowing are identical.

"Yes, I'm not surprised," she said when I took the lighter-than-air souvenir scrap from its case. "Got it from an old woman's estate over in 'The Corners.' Looked like the kind of thing someone like you would like. Normally, I can't give that crap away."

"Always call the customer an asshole," she might have added, but didn't, except in my mind, where I heard it clearly.

Then:

"Would you take thirty-five for this?" I asked her.

"No."

"Fifty?

"Well, if I have to."

I held my prize with as much restrained eagerness as I could muster, just to see that look on her face: the look anyone gets when they suddenly suspect that hey! someone might know something you don't, is about to profit from it at your expense, and it's too late to undo the deal.

"I'd have paid the seventy-five, you stupid butt-sucking hag," I might have added, but didn't, except in my mind, where I spoke it clearly.

Luckily for me, it was a fifty-dollar silent insult to a grounded emancipation, and I'll now never have to imagine an Honest Abe almost fourteen miles high, ballooning around in a stovepipe football helmet, getting through the winter on nothing but Mary Todd's hardtack and the hidden musings of a dead humorist.

I am sympathetic, however, that you will.

R.G.B.
Spring 2010

IN WATERMELON SALT

B. Elwin Sherman

IN WATERMELON SALT

With death just around the corner, I'm now free to tell you that the only name I ever heard and remembered in an introduction was my own.

Much earlier in my life, whenever I entered a roomful of new faces and my host passed me from one namesayer to the next, I nodded, smiled and moved on, forgetting every name as I heard it. If I later had to speak with any of them, I was obliged to again smile and blurt: "And, YOU are?"

Sometimes in re-introductions this happened simultaneously, as both of us scrambled to remember:

""**A**-a **N**-n **D**-d,, **Y**-y-**O**-o-**U**-u **A**-a-**R**-r-**E**-e??""

This mutual voiceover immediately started my counterpart thinking metaphysically, like some mind-melding pre-connection had just happened between us.

This is psychodramatic bullshit.

Human beings don't have this capacity, though they'd give you an argument about it, and I've never given it a second thought until today.

Somehow, knowing that I'll soon be compost has a way of fertilizing old foregone conclusions.

Sometimes, despite an ocean of odds against it, we're nothing more than the MS Stockholm and the SS Andrea Doria of conversation. One of us never sees the other one coming and always sinks as the result, though we don't realize it at the time.

One doesn't sink, and continues to operate as a cruise ship. One does, and then must always serve as a permanent reef. Now there's the thumbnail history of men & women.

Let's not make a big mystery of it. It's not.

Don't waste your time wondering about the causes and effects of rare disasters or common happenstance. You'll go crazy, and before you know it, your thoughts will trickle down into worrying about things you shouldn't worry about, like when two Volvos collide on the interstate. Was it due to their unique metallurgical affinity? Was there a Volvovian carjink driver destiny at work?

I'm not kidding. There are everyday people out there whose everyday brains have devolved into an every-third-day kind of thinking like this about everything, and worse.

And, worse still, the further you stray from fatalism, the more you'll also not worry about things that you should worry about. The problem there is you won't know it until the worse happens. In this life we live, I like those scenarios the best.

I once heard a comedian suggest that tornadoes are caused by trailer parks. Now, there are minds which not only don't find the humor in that, but think it plausible, as if concentrated amounts of aluminum, beer and semen can stir an atmospheric dust-up in Quonset hut cooperatives, just as there are real people who believe that Volvos and Volvo drivers can have it in for each other.

There are some real mother-loving idiots in this world.

A once living great American humorist now dead from drink said: "There are no lengths to which humorless people will not go to analyze Humor." I think that's what killed him, not the alcohol.

Cirrhosis can't beat self-indulgence as a terminal disease.

If we accept that we can have the same thought at the same instant as someone else and sometimes happen to speak it at that same instant, but we believe the reason for this is because we're somehow preordained as soulmates fused together by cosmic solder, then we're as cracked as the vehicular and mobile home whirlwind karma people.

I once heard a conversation with this kind of co-blurt between two introductees. They were of opposite sexes, and that was reason enough, that night, in their condition, and all other appearances aside, to spark their libidos. Plus, the hour was late, and their first, second and third choices hadn't panned out. I know, because I'd watched them pan in.

They wanted to believe this last-call connection predestinate, rather than a natural process of elimination, an orderly thinning of the last-call human herd as it then descended into the following exchange (they'd been agreeing that, yes, history was some kind of revolving sequel written just for them):

""**Y**-y-**O**-o-**U**-u,, **T**-t-**O**-o-**O**-o??"" they co-queried, sealing the end of their future together, at least past the next morning, when their false-positive orphic notions would be trumped by bed hair, bad breath and the wrong coffee.

"Yeah! I've always felt like I was Mark Antony on Cleopatra's barge in another life. It's weird!"

"REALLY? WOW! And I've always felt like I was Cleopatra!"

I repeat: this is never true, and should be abandoned on the spot, especially if she looks nothing like Elizabeth Taylor and he has motion sickness and no sword. Like rivers and myths and social diseases, the origins of lust should never be revealed, much less revisited.

I haven't always followed this rule.

I'm not following it now.

But, the whole thing pains me, because I know something about people that people don't know about themselves:

I know that in the same instant two lovers say their first Hellos, they are already practicing their Goodbyes. Oh, not so either notices the other doing it, but in the deep recesses of mortal self-definitions also best kept quiet, like embarrassing Vaudeville afflictions:

(Upstage) Hello! I have Irritable Bowel Syndrome and I can't dance.

(Downstage) Goodbye! I have no sweat glands and I can't sing.

Offstage, I can never say Hello without feeling like I've at least implied permission to be trampled.

Hellos are little more than no-talent Goodbyes in secret dress rehearsal: anonymous method actors in the right acts and the wrong plays.

But, I also loathe Goodbyes, which is why I've lived in secret like this and written like this and avoided Hellos for so long.

You will find some scraps of connective tissue in the little stories that follow. It will create the impression that in the now quarter-plus century I've been thought dead, I've been alive and in analytical concert with what I've experienced.

Don't you believe it. Most of this later life has just washed over me. I'm not dead yet, but life will soon fix that.

Come some fast-approaching sundown, I'll be as dead as the sweeteners mother Lulu used to keep in her little porcelain watermelon salt & pepper shakers.

She stored the saccharin in watermelon pepper, and the sugar in watermelon salt.

That's about how this life has gone.

JILL VONNEGUT'S FORD 04/11/07

I didn't have to do what I've done.

I might've written travel guides, or fashion catalogue copy, or compacted op/ed pieces for rural weeklies. I could've been a country song lyricist, or a cereal jinglist, or king of the office temp memos, if I hadn't hated offices more than Hello-Goodbyes. Only fate kept me from writing what I'll call "Shims."

These days, Shims sell well, buy their authors at least the runner-up couch spots in talk-show circuits, and always smack of being someone else's recipe in a rejacketed textbook.

"His latest book: '*LIBERALS WITHOUT LASSITUDE* – *The De-ReEnergization Of Left-Wing Poobah,'* is to neo-nonconformity what cow dung is to---"

You get the picture. Blockbusters.

Interchangeable pulp. Mostly whiny, slick without cleverness, and often exposed in the end as unoriginal and plagiarized, which only seems to sell more Shims and bump their creators from second guest banana sofas into the exclusive talk-show comfy chairs, including the follow-up mea culpas good for another million book buyers looking to avenge their own gullibility by making these authors richer.

We Americans love self-inflicted wounds.

Best-selling books have become the literary equivalents of automobile cloning: No distinctive lines, the same three rotating dull shades of dark and off-dark Confederate blues & utility greens, over-optionalized interiors and cloned exteriors.

It's as if the motorcars of America have forgotten an old man's glory days, mis-recalled an old woman's cookie cutter, and bypassed a child's toy stove.

It makes me feel sad and lonely, and like someone who more and more finds less and less difference between arriving and leaving. Might as well be dead, when either moving or sitting motionless yields the same results.

Isn't that plain enough? History will record, if history is paying attention, that I at least posed the question right here.

When I chance to see an old surviving Mustang or a Camaro or even a Corvair or Volkswagen Beetle, (the real heater-less kind) I feel like Kurt Vonnegut, Jr. has just driven by in an all-wheel drive Bagombo Snuff Box.

I love that name, and have always thought that Ford should've used it as a new model. It was wasted as a book title, even if it was now God-damn dead ahead of me Kurt Vonnegut, Jr.'s.

"The all-new Ford Bagombo -- Built Slaughterhouse Five-By-Five Snuff Box Tough."

I wonder if Jill can drive a standard shift.

AUSTRALIAN BAGPIPES

Out loud, I'd said it:

What Bagpipe Annie desperately needed to hear that night.

I called her Bagpipe Annie because she was the only woman I'd ever met who played the bagpipes. When we first made love I found it erotic as hell, though I couldn't begin to explain why. I'm sure it touched some clever composer's chord of arousal somewhere in my thinking, stirring up something about the seduction of discord, the horny, strap-on urges that certain dissonances spark---but that's enough of that crap and about as far as I want to blueprint it.

It didn't matter, because a month later, whatever sexy image her bagpiping first drafted in my mind had been erased and replaced with the sensation that my teeth were constantly dripping blood.

So, out loud, I'd said it:

"I'm going out, Lover. But, before I go, has anyone told you today about your raven hair, wildfire fingers, your sensitive, commanding eyes, infectious laugh and the trilateral festival of your ass?"

That's what I'd said out loud.   Trouble is, it came out sounding like: "I'm going out."

So, she left me, and left me a note:

Bedmouth, my love,

So, where have you been?   Wallowing in sludge in the harbor? Groping at a dwarf?   Panting lacsiviously (sp?) at ten-year olds by the drugstore?   Abusing yourself while watching Mary Popping? (Actually, that's more a Freudian slip than a typo)

Anyway, old thing, why don't you come upstairs and let me tap dance on your temples or fondle your backbone whilst whistling the chorus from a star is born or play tiddlywinks on your genitalia with a goose feather dipped in olive oil?

Kindest Regards,
The Bareassed Contessa

That's what she'd written.   Trouble is, it came out reading like bloody teeth:

So, where have you been?
You know what? I don't care!
Don't write.
Don't call.
Don't exist.
Kindly leave the fucking planet.
                    ---A.

So, she left me and left me her spongy snapalastic slippers, the one made for those tiny feet, stretchable to U-Boat EEE.

They were laughing at me from the couch, huddling in the cushion-crack like green burned kangaroo pouches.

And then, like a spoiled rotten boomerang, Emily Dickinson herself came crashing back in, swooping though the front door.

"I died," she swooped, "for beauty."

"Dead is dead," I said. "So, get out and take your pouches and bagpipes with you."

Snap.

Snap.

Drip.

Slam.

THE CHINESE CAVALRY MASSACRE

I've known women whose names I've forgotten but whose faces and bodies I remember. I've known other women whose cars, apartments, even phones & license plate numbers and sisters-in-law I recall, but whose images are just a blur, like fallen trees with their bottoms still attached to shore but their tops now half-submerged in a swift, muddy river.

But, I've never met a woman who I could later remember the whole of -- with only a few exceptions. If I've done this right, there should be four:

1. If we'd met before, in THIS LIFE, (I kept my incarnate pick-up lines in the mock mystic where they belonged) and both of us hadn't forgotten why or how. Remembering the when or where of a thing is never very important.

It's the whys and hows in this life that will get you killed or laid.

I may have that backwards. I'll leave that to you.

I do know that no one is ever in the wrong place at the wrong time, or the right place at the right time, or the wrong place at the right time, or the right place at the wrong time. That's where I stand with Divine Intervention.

It's a mandatory game of Russian roulette for conscientious objectors.

2. If either of us owed money to someone the other knew.

3. If, at the moment we met, a piano fell through the floor.

4. If not a plummeting piano, then something else interesting presented itself: an errant bodily function involving at least two of the senses, a cat running between us with its tail on fire, a solar or lunar eclipse, the self-assassination of someone worthy of being publicly murdered by someone else -- something we both then and forever could never forget, and would always associate with only each other.

Only then, for me, would a name and a face connect, and remain connected.

Only then ... could I say Goodbye.

When she first said Hello-Goodbye, she smiled and took my outstretched hand as if she was lifting the corner of a sleeping baby's heirloom blanket. At once, I felt both attracted to and repelled by her because she wasn't evasive with her eyes and she knew how to leave when she arrived, yet she still shook my hand as I expected, the way most women do with men, especially the beautiful ones, which she was.

Shaking hands with a beautiful woman has always made me feel ill. My hand afterward feels like it has just given the coupé de grace to a mortally wounded bird. A chickadee, let's say.

Let's say chickadees, because they're one of the few birds who'll tough-out a Northeast winter as their bigger-bodied brethren beat it out of here. Mercy killings should be reserved for little heroes.

Blue jays and crows can kiss my ass.

I'll miss California.

I also believe that our body parts can and often do direct their own destinies. Who among us has not had a reluctant knee, an overzealous shoulder, a forgetful penis, an avenging vagina? (You may mix and match any of those modifiers to any of those nouns, and cite examples of each. Try it. I'll wait.)

Our bodies are what would happen if the people at Cracker Jack made one big Pandora's Chinese Box and placed tiny reproductions of them in new uteruses with the prizes removed. Just that visual alone, when all other reasoning failed me, has more than once kept me from sticking my head in a vise.

But, sticking my head in a vise, so far, has also presented me with a special problem: it needs an accomplice to succeed (at least the kind of success I look for when I'm shopping for surefire obliteration). I may have chosen not to choose this method because of that. It's a hard thing to ask of a friend.

It's also my way of giving myself a flawed ultimatum.

Thoughts like that are probably why I should've had a therapist all this time, and I almost did once with her (the woman who went when she came and took my hand like an old treasured bunting). But, when we were on our way to that first therapy, the therapist chose that afternoon to kill herself.

To this day, I can't feel badly about that. It made me feel like a soldier who'd escaped vivisection at the Little Big Horn by hiding under a dead horse.

Sometimes a woman shook my hand like a man, but that made me feel worse, because women cannot shake hands like men, and when they try, they shake hands like women trying to shake hands like men. When I got this kind of handshake from a woman, it was my hand's turn to feel like it had been put out of its misery.

It's best for men and women to not shake hands when they first meet.

Touching foreheads might work.

Or, elbows. Or, elbows to foreheads.

But, no hands. Hands do too much else to be so devalued in such sincere pretenses. Shared hands should never be cordial. They should create or destroy, hard-labor anonymously or excite in the spotlight, deliver or take life. Hands were meant for high drama or low deeds.

Consider the thumb: Its saddle joint alone should have its own museum. A full-fingered hand without a thumb cannot make a fist, but a thumb with only one of the remaining digits can hold its own against any fully-fingered clencher.

True enough, flautists finding themselves so-affected might then be reduced to performing only diatonic compositions, but this is alright with me. Half-notes and flute song are like having too many varieties of mustard on hand when you really want ketchup.

Without a thumb, fingers alone can't light a match. Add the thumb, and voila! A thumb and a pinky can lift a bowling ball. Index finger and pinky? A silly, partial pincer, as useful as half a crab. Can't even masturbate without cramping, and I'm not ashamed to admit that I've determined that fact through hands-on research. No sacrifice too small for you.

Hands should be heroic or cowardly, never neutral or cautious. Switzerland would be a poor excuse for a hand, even if it had Germany for a wrist. Ireland would be a bejeweled handshake in rubber gloves, and America would be an oven mitt with no hand at all.

I'll stop this metaphor at the Canadian border, which would have no fingerprints. We won't bother about Mexico, which would use its feet.

Toes, on the other hand, should stay hidden, brought out only for deviations in the dark, walking in sand, scratching a dog's belly or turning on a dime, but they shouldn't make a nickel argument out of it. They should not make a fuss. Yes, they are largely responsible for balance, grace and agility, but they needn't lord it under you. I don't know one woman who loves the sight of her toes or one man who uses his wisely.

Toes have been my foot's sin-eaters and my leg's altar boys.

Hands were my Ten Commandments and seven deadly sins.

Apparently, that made my pelvis a defrocked priest.

When my baby blanket baby left me for a Soft Rock disc jockey, I couldn't have done worse by her if I'd taken up sides against a Chinese Custer's battle plan, with my diminishing empty boxes all hurriedly stuffed into one lucky chickenshit horse soldier's saddlebags.

CHEERLEADING IN
MIDWESTERN NORWAY

Here's another true story about thumbs and toes and healthcare in America that contradicts the one you just read. That's what I love about life and love even more than the prospect of death.

There are opposite rules to every exception. Even this one.

Once true upon another time, two people whose names wouldn't help you just yet were married. That's also what I love about this story. Armed here with only a few details about their entire lives, you'll have all the information you'll need to feel like you've known them all of yours.

Today, you're one lucky reader. I'd trade places with you.

The man, a Midwesterner of common character, had his uncommon thumb blown off not long after the blessed union, and the doctors had replaced it (thumb) with his great toe.

It had taken a team of two doctors – one limb detachment specialist and one limb reattachment specialist – to respectively disassemble and reassemble the man's appendages.

Later, a boatload of them from either camp couldn't have saved the marriage. Scalpels and bone saws are no match for good hot-curvy loving gone flat-cold bad.

As an interesting sidebar, (knowing how much you love distractions with covert motives) you might take a moment to consider how the machinery of modern medicine is made to work in opposites and contradictions. Here, let me help you:

A branch of medicine over HERE relieves THAT, but its root sister's side effects over THERE cause THOSE. To treat THEM, you need another kind of THIS, which generates a mutated form of THESE, and on, and so on, EVERYWHERE.

That's enough. You'll have to find your own accents the rest of the way, but be careful; don't mistake volume for pitch. As the humorist, that's been my license. As the reader, you have to keep me closer than that.

Somewhere in this caducean crapshoot, surgeons usually take over and insurance companies start denying claims.

American healthcare has too many greedy pronouns, each one looking to profit itself on the cheap, and it can never discuss the one truth that would kill it in a minute: healing and curing should never move in with each other. Healing and curing are the dog people and cat people of all human wellness.

No wonder we're all a little sick with some febrile degree of this or that indisposition all of the time. No wonder we all live like dogs and try to act like cats.

Save the nuances; I'll yield the point ahead of time.

Life … life is … life is like … (you'll also hear this a lot from me now, because looming death has a way of pushing a puffed-up introspection ahead of it, as the last tide wedges the last piece of driftwood into its very last unlikely tossed-up crook).

Damn it. I hope that just because I'll be dead soon I don't go too heavy on the metaphors. Fast-approaching mortality does seem to provoke a duck n' cover muse, but I'll try to minimize it.

Life is very much like … a medicine cabinet full of expired anti-probiotics that you can't throw out, even after the illnesses they were meant to treat are way past resolved by recovery or death, usually in spite of the medicines.

Care for a harsher, simpler, profounder metaphor? Me too:

Modern medicine is like a crazy traitorous general sending stone soldiers into gun battles with broken swords after the armistice.

Even knowing this, we still can't trash our useless remedies because, unlike myths, synergy is the last thing to go in this life, not hearing. You already know why you can't toss out a hardened heart's desires, and you don't need a washed-up, holed-up old prosodist/curmudgeon on the brink of extinction to lecture you about it.

It's for the same reasons you can't bring yourself to surrender that gaudy carnival neck bauble, (the one you won for her that she wore just to please you that night) or that crude attempt at a first love letter (the one he sent to your sickbed when you hadn't even known he was longing for you).

Now, if I know how you feel, and you wouldn't be here if I didn't, this has been just enough digression to bring your thumb-toe tale curiosity to a boil.

Down there on the end of his foot, the surgery left our Heartlander a little off-balance, and with a permanent slight limp. Up there on the end of his arm he had a passable fist, but his hand wasn't happy about it because it had become incapable of uncommon work or play.

At this point, it wouldn't change this story if I told you that he'd lost his thumb when his brother blew it off in a hunting accident that involved an argument over the latter's boot laces, so I'll save that for the end.

I also can't remember if thumb and toe were on our hero's dominant side, so we'll just exclude that tidbit altogether. Remember, we're throwing out the incidentals today. This is bare bones raconteuring.

Here's the rub: Before the shooting, even though the man himself was forgettable, his uncommon thumb had done the most titillating things to his wife, and in places she herself had long-thought dead until he and his savant hand arrived.

In their all sexied-up heyday, even when she couldn't arouse him, even when he was sleeping and wouldn't wake up, she could convince his thumb, along with its phalangeal cohorts, to work its erotic magic without him.

Again, I know the names of the man and his wife, even the doctors, the hospital and the host city, but you needn't feel deprived if I continue to omit them. They are not the most significant characters in this story, despite the following evidence:

After her husband's accident and affixation, (he called it his "big piggie paw") she found that the great toe cum thumb had corrupted its neighbors, and, try as she might, she couldn't get any of them to satisfy her. Not one tap, twirl or sweeping motion. Not a tickle or a tweak. The new mitt couldn't find her G-Spot if it had an alphabetical Norwegian road map, and "G" was the only rest stop between Fauske and Hokksund.

Before, inside her, his hand and its agents, with thumb leading the charge, had acted like they were Odin The Wanderer and she was an erotic Runic alphabet, and any hand able to masquerade as Norse mythology in search of a hot Germanic language knew the way to her heart, even if its owner was a Iowan hog farmer.

One day, the new hand ran off with Birdie (a name I will now name, because she has, after all, just become the critical character here, and it will help you visualize an Ottumwan manicurist with a pierced tongue and a foot fetish).

I'm glad it was Ottumwa and I'm glad I've chosen this moment to reveal this. It wasn't easy keeping that to myself, because "Ottumwa" is one of those words that can tie together a story's loose ends all along the way without meaning to. Its harsh and lounging syllables allows you to forgive throwaway yet nagging details, but I'm always obliged to leave you at least a pretense of discretionary labor beyond a simple word scan.

As we've agreed, if I let you become a lazy reader, I'd also slip into slothful composition and you'd blame me for it. I prefer to make no apologies and to enjoy not expressing them while I'm still alive.

Plus, I like saying it, if only in my head. Ottumwa. Ottumwa. Ottumwa. Ahhh.

Fuck this, I'm saying it out loud. "Ottumwa! OH! TUM! WAH!"

In fact:

They lived upstairs in a rented, Ottumwatian shoebox (amazing how one good shout can expand a qualifier).

This is where you don't need me. You now know damn well what the rest of Birdie looked like.

Today, the hand -- with a living prosthetic big toe for a dead thumb -- writes alimony checks on Scandinavian religious holidays. The signature is halting, but legible.

Birdie fumes over this as she waits in the shoebox, doing her nails and dressed in the hand-me-down team sweater of a Gangstadhaugen cheerleading floozy.

Finally, I've just decided that I won't be telling you his name. It doesn't go well with Birdie, and I won't have you upset over it. I can't allow you to leave here feeling like you'd feel if you'd just been asked to believe that there once was a real Renaissance couple named Isabella Rossellini and Bucky Dent.

Then again, given how this ends, that's probably exactly what you should feel.

The End: The brother never laced up his hunting boots properly, even though our philandering toe-in-hand prosthetician had repeatedly needled him about it when they went hunting together.

Yes, you're right, that's what happened:

Inevitably, while crossing a stone fence, he stepped on the loose lace, tripped, pitched forward and discharged his rifle into his nagging brother's foot, forever annexing Norway and Iowa.

Oh, and what about the future of healthcare in America?

Forget that.

SAMANTHA'S SWEARING-OUT CEREMONY

It didn't matter that Samantha knew, as did I, how to leave before she arrived. I still felt about her the same way I felt about any nursing woman's breasts:

Milk pumps or erotic toys?

I've always been confused and felt awkward by my desire to have both, as both, for myself.

Something has always been wrong with me on that score: to want what a child needs, and need what a child wants, mixed in with grown-up ulterior motives

Those little mad misfires are the only real parts of me left that I enjoy anymore. I tell myself I'm correct: an old man should be reduced to having only a few remaining snippets of both his own familiarity and contempt that he can abide, and fewer still that give him any pleasure, with the fewest of all being the ones he's not aware of, or would prefer not to think about.

If my life was an old man metaphor, I'd be the nursing home confinee always escaping to the lobby with his full urinal, bent upon killing the lobby's house plant centerpiece, the unnatural-looking one that you can't tell if it's real or manufactured without touching, and even then you're not sure.

Waxy, floppy leaves and polished bark, looking more dead alive than it ever does alive dead. You remember. It's how your great-grandfather looked in his coffin when you were forced to tell him you loved him out loud in public and had to give him that ghastly goodbye kiss as a child.

On second thought, I don't belong anywhere on either side of that metaphor, unless the lobby has a concert grand player piano in it.

I tell myself that my long-dead therapist would have approved of that thinking, if she hadn't been so afraid of death that she'd killed herself. She might've even been entertained long enough by my funhouse mirror-image version of Mother Nurture versus Father Nature to have postponed, if not entirely redirected, her own execution. We'll never know.

This is contradiction: a practice I've long admired and employed with words only. I never wanted people's behaviors to be in opposition. Not in front of me. It made me feel uneasy, and if they came from a disarming beauty like Samantha?

Nauseated on the spot.

If she was going to look at me like that, so accusatorily, then her handshake should've reflected the accusation. She should have grabbed my hand like the salesman does when you agree to sign the contract, not the way he does when you're standing there fuming three months later complaining about your ding-bang transmission

But, because she was a woman, it would've been a saleswoman impersonating a salesman's phony handshake. We've discussed this. No good.

Is there a solution?

Not without inserting another asynchronous story right here, and I think that you've already had just about enough of that. Let's just leave it that men, women and vehicles were never all meant to comingle, certainly not to the degree that we have. The result has always been a seriocomic mêlée, like two wild animals fighting over an empty can of beans.

None of this locked Samantha's name into my face, however. It was when, as we first took hands after she spoke and before we let go -- and I turned and threw up on the shoes of the man to my left, overcome with the realization that I was a man trapped in a man's body, and recoiling there before me was the dazzling sameness of a self-opposing woman I knew I'd be in bed with before midnight -- that forever defined her first gentle clutch as our start/finish line.

A year later, in fact, when my past with her arrived, it was her closing rant as she went out the door for the last time:

"Charles should've thrown up on YOU! FUCKSCUMMER!"

Pardon my construction, but you need to understand how it didn't help that I laughed right there when Samantha swore at me. Laughing at and during another person's rage always spells doom, but she'd just never mastered the art of the expletive, always adopting understated or mismatched parts or belaboring the obvious, and you can't beat half-baked cussing for hilarity.

Other examples? Dicktinsel! Shitforguts! Now I can feel your sympathy, and don't think I'm not grateful.

Then, I remembered:

Charles. The stranger to my left.

""A-a N-n D-d,, Y-y-O-o-U-u A-a-R-r-E-e??""

Charles couldn't have presented less like a future gigolo. He was proof that some human beings have the power to immediately send your stomach into trebuchet mode, just by showing up. He wore mismatched high-topped sneakers of different colors that I topped with partially digested finger foods – the right footwear for a color-blind bowery seer, not a word-wrapped girlfriend's secret paramour.

THE BOSTON-TO-SAN FRANCISO
BIBLE STUDY

"Just once, do you think you could cook an egg without---"

In this high-speed daydream, it was the only known case of a man going to the gallows dead, and with his neck already broken.

It's also helpful here for you to know that when my mind wandered on that Haight Street apartment morning, it did so with proper nouns, an elaborate fairy tale, and in the time it took a scorched scrambled egg to travel across a kitchen.

Scorpion Pete.

AKA Clarence Corona. An odd offspring of a transplanted Eastern widowed maternity and a thoroughly Western wandering polecat paternity. Mama was a lady and Papa was a buckaroo. The damsel and the drunk. Right vs. might.

Clarence became Scorpion Pete when, at fifteen-years old – a pale, sickly excuse of a son in the eyes of his hellraising Daddy and a painfully shy, gentle treasure in his Mother's heart – he

40

was tossed from the saddle on his way home from school into a resting nest of scorpion. Bitten and nearly died so many times, the Doc said, the venom just stayed in his blood.

Never was the same after that.

Whopped his liquored up old man on the head with a hot branding iron about a month later. Came out of nowhere, for no reason, and as the pistol-packing patriarch sprawled in the dust, gazing through daze and drink at this son of his gone loco, Clarence took the hot thing and burned a Lazy S into his stupefied father's chin, then left him to die in the heat, walked into the house and seared a five-thousand dollar Wanted Dead Or Alive reward into the hands that rocked the cradle Corona.

When the local lawmen finally got to him he'd turned seven men and three women into New Mexico mincemeat. All killed from behind. All left with a Lazy S somewhere on their person. Carved, drawn or branded.

At the hanging, a small crowd waited, mostly relatives of the decreased.

"Any last words, my son?" asked the parson.

Personally, the parson didn't give a sweet mesquite what the damnable delinquent had to say. The local schoolmarm had been the parson's lover. Had been, until he found her -- head and arms clamped inside a desk, a Lazy S sliced into her spread-eagled bloomers. On the blackboard had been scrawled:

Skopian Pete
Clas of 1900

41

When the dime novels and newspapers back East recounted this, they'd corrected the spelling. For some reason, they wanted their parricidal anti-heroes to be literate.

By giving Pete an opportunity to deliver his own verbal epitaph, the parson maintained humility and grace in the face of the hellish outlaw and the gathering of the faithful and suspended disbelievers, though you could tell by his white-knuckled grip on the Bible and the suppressed yelping cries from the crowd, that his avenging blood lust was raring to go.

The Book of Matthew, Chapter Five, Verse 38 was itching for affirmation.

Verse 39 could go jump in the Red Sea.

Scorpion Pete, hands tied behind, took one step forward to the edge of the gallows and looked down at the riveted assembly:

"I may be going up the flume, but I feel fine as cream gravy." These were hard-riding Western colloquialisms, even then. Sensing trouble, the sheriff reached for him. About to lose his composure, the parson dropped the Bible.

"Take this as sound on the goose: NEVER count on nothing happenin' the way you plan it," Pete said, grinning.

Again, the Eastern redactors changed this to "something happening" (double negatives and an informal tone in their cutthroat heathen headliners would also not do).

"More'n likely you'll end up sure as some fuckin' surprised."

In the Baltimore Daily News, this was reported as "You'll be amazed." The Schenectady Sun quoted: "You'll know what I meant." The Cleveland Courier had him speechless altogether. They'd all had just about enough of profane, borderline analphabetic and grammatically untidy killers. From there on out, the fiction writers took over.

The parson bowed his head and Scorpion Pete sidekicked him below the Bible belt, sending him to his knees taking the Lord's name, along with the rest of the family's, in serious vain.

"JESUSMARYANDJOSEPH!"

He bent over his fallen Bible like the eternally sad baseball legacy of Bill Buckner.   Pete dodged out of the sheriff's grasp and ran up and off the parson's back and over the railing.

Sitting alone in the rapidly undercrowding kitchen, a burned and scrambled egg grazed the aircastling humorist's right ear, and he was left hanging for dead at the breakfast table.

"----incinerating it?"

RUTH JUDGES
THE NONFICTION HUMOR NOVELIST

I can't remember if I dreamed that I imagined this, or imagined that I dreamt it, night or day.

There were I think herbal hallucinogenics responsible for this confusion, along with a woman named Ruth, an unnamed man, and someone acting suspiciously like me arguing over a cheating lover. I also remember dogs, lots of dogs, and a long circuitous trip in a car with right-hand drive.

It's not important that you know where this originated. It's even less important that I remember, but if this is one of those days where you can't budge without a formal introduction, use this:

On the day Ruth left me, somewhere in my mind I was called up for civic duty as Truman Capote, something any humorist would die for.

Have you formed any opinions, Mr. Capote, regarding the charges brought forth against this defendant?

Observations, perhaps.

Would you elaborate, please?

Ironic horror. Vice-ridden prodigies. Religious Mayhem. Cracks in the door. Untimely tire punctures. Bullet cook-off's. Poisonous beauty. Inanimate fright. Sexual weapons. Inventive matricides. Irreverent bodily functions. Computerized audacity. Anonymous revenge. Runaway coffins. Justifiable terrorism. Living nightmares. Post-ordained victims. Midgets. Brain-damaged offspring locked in basements. Lemmings. Cannibals. Self-hypnosis. This voir dire. Enough?

You're intrigued by these things?

They appeal to me.

In what ways?

A medical student named Detierre, in the spirit of post-war patriotic egoism, once injected himself with insect serum almost certainly known to be deadly. He did this hoping to disprove a medical truism based on research done by those living under the opposing flag.

And?

He died in agony.

You consider that relevant to this case?

I consider that hilarious.

And, the other things you mentioned. Examples?

A distraught man attempts to immolate himself. But, as the fire ignites he loses his courage and rolls around frantically trying to smother the flames. He falls from a nearby precipice to his death. A pleading, plummeting, human fireball. Painfully funny.

Go on.

A car rams into a parked tanker. Explodes. Burns. When it's over, the driver's left hand, clamped on to the outside mirror, is all that remains recognizable. A reliable indication that he'd been looking backwards as he was getting killed frontwards. A common, yet largely unheralded phenomenon.

Others?

The aging film actress released from her contract, going berserk and dismembering the family cat, then tidily wrapping and mailing the various limbs and viscera to several studio executives. The diet expert dying of malnutrition. The author of a best-selling book on running, running into a surprise ending. The nervous liquor store thief clumsily blowing a hole in his chest with his own revolver. The notion of a constipated cleric. The notion of a constipated cleric remedy. The porno publisher proclaiming piety. The scuba diver attempting to break the world depth record, drowning when he lost his breakfast.

You keep an account of these things?

I remember them. I seek them out when it's convenient. I research them when it's profitable. I invent some, experiment with others.

You experiment with them? Hypothetically?

No.

Would you tell the Court, Mr. Capote, just how these -- observations -- affect your ability to render an impartial verdict in this case?

No such thing exists.

What?

Only THOUGHT can be impartial. An ACTION, or verdict as it applies here, whether decisive or flimsy, fair or unfair, clean or dirty, popular or not, must lose any cloak of neutrality by virtue of its effect, or lack of it thereof, upon the receiver.

Have you yourself ever been the victim of a crime?

Not until this moment.

Are you saying---?

I'm saying that if your client, with his attorney as counter-weight, were both gibbeted from Lady Justice this very moment, I would not take offense. Short of that, I'm saying that his scrotum should be nailed to the floor, and that a rusty nail and a few missed hammer strikes would seem neither cruel nor unusual to me.

The Defense challenges this Juror, Madam Judge.

WHEN JUANITA DUMPED
JACK KEROUAC

You deserve to have this story's two-part moral right up front:

Part One: Half of a two lovers' love epitaph is better than none.

Part Two: On the eve of a break-up with a hot-tempered woman, never read from *The Subterraneans*, then lie down for a nap with a bellyful of Mexican take-out.

Three days after he'd suffocated on his working dinner chimichanga---

Three days after the Mexicano fast-food magnate was struck down in mid-sentence at 12:30 p.m., a most inopportune moment for his three riveted dinner companions because of where he'd been with them contractually at the height of his last raised and drawn syllable, when spiced chicken met his suddenly synchronized co-conspirators of gag reflex, acid reflux, and the synapse miscues sparked by the huddled-down proximity of Juanita, the densely perfumed buxom waitress---

Three days after she attempted to dislodge the jammed peppermill crank and target-ratchet it, leaning into the quadwranglers for optimum tip-padding exposure with the always-auditioning flair common to any unagented harlequin waitress so-endowed in the upper cleft, and instead broke the thing just as his promised commitment to the co-investing triune was forever prematurely choked on the threshold of an aspirated proposition, prompted by, as we've already belabored, not only his autonomic misroutings but the sight of peppercorns cascading into that patchouli upper valley of the doll-faced table thespian when her topheavy torque bottomed-out the burlesque millworks, the sight of which suckheld the startled chairman's fowl chimi-chunk in a tracheal throttle worthy of a Goldbergian diagram---

Three days after this blue-facing burrito king, eyes agog in desperate alarm, pounded his fist into a bowl of borracho beans and slammed headlong into the pork rinds, catapulting a curlicue crumb-shower aloft and down upon the startled party like a waning fireworks display, and before he back-vaulted the tabletop with his knees into what one witness later described as "a giant, slow-motion tiddlywink with legs"---

Three days after companion # 1, temporarily blinded by the refried bean shrapnel, stumbled away from the scene and impaled his palm on the cashier's toothpick caddy, rendering whatever incapable assistance he might have offered an afterdinner thought---

Three days after companion # 2, thinking this was either a psychosocial crisis over merger addendums, (was it the labor dispute line-item?) cursingly beat a skittering nonsecularturned-Tartuffian retreat to the men's room, replete with a shitfuck borracho bean flapping atop his Christly pissbitch left ear---

Three days after companion # 1, a man who knew an oafish but windless wizard and a fast-retreating acquisition when he saw them, fell upon the former, Heimlich at the ready, and too-high only managed to break the breastbone of the cyanosing deal breaker, whose paroxysmal silence was also rapidly quieting any promise that the submerging Southwestern expansion agreement would then ever find its way into their desert stopovers, beginning with his, a recently acquired and only marginally solvent pornographic publishing franchise on west Tucson's Miracle Mile---

Three days after Juanita the hysterical condiment hostess (remember her?) under-dramatized the entire act by sweeping peppercorns from her exposed embonpoints, not yet questioning, as she later would, her absent gratuity and premier role, or lack of it, as the table's provocateuress---

Three days later, and the sign still hung on his (my) abandoned apartment door:

(In Spanish):

"OUT TO LUNCH. BACK AT ONE."

BAZAAR CAT

I once watched a woman watch her husband die. Most of the logistics and supporting cast of that experience don't matter. As I've mentioned, at this stage in the old breathe-in, breathe-out, I'm trying to minimize your clutter, too.

Be still, now. The following things do matter:

Without a word, she went immediately to the bedroom closet and began rearranging his suits on the hangers.

If you've ever seen a cat in the middle of a wet lawn forced to pick-step its way through the grass, then you've wondered why and how it would ever walk out there in the first place.

Keep that image and that wonder in your mind now, because that's the way she walked over to the closet full of his dead clothes then.

After we saw him breathe his last, either she did that and was allowed to do that, or she would've run screaming into the street. In her immersion into grief, she immediately found the means to breathe underwater. Eons of back-adaptation taking hold in the absence of a breath.

She'd had been better served right then, however, if she'd spent more time in her life watching mad cats walk on wet grass.

Ack! Too late. We only get the one chance to rewrite history.

In shock, and unaware there was any alternative, or even having the ability to imagine one might exist, she walked over to that foolish closet like a cat learning the hard way that it didn't only rain on dog day afternoons, and dedicated herself to not screaming at her dead husband's dead clothes.

Everything in there was dead. Everything in there had never been alive. Even the wooden hangers were counterfeit.

I stood next to her, as her lifelong partner remained dead in the middle of the room. I'd seen lots of dead men before, but she hadn't. It was a new script for her, but he couldn't have played his role any better.

We stood together quietly, re-mixing and matching his freshly disowned clothes. She handed me a suit from one end of the rack, and I re-hung it on the other end. This had no clear meaning, which is why it was the perfect and necessary thing to do.

Already, the suit felt and hung like a dead man's suit, as if it had poured out its occupant, rather than the other usual method.

She turned and moved over to the dresser. I followed her, doing my best to wet grass-walk like an annoyed cat on the verge of losing its cat cool.

Nothing is cooler than cat cool, so you know how fragile I felt.

We silently performed similar labors with his underwear. End-to-end briefs. End-to-end tee-shirts. One drawer to the next. From there to there. Meaningless tasks done alone, but with one vital motivation put together.

I said nothing to her. That's one of life's little secrets and something the dead have always tried to teach us: knowing when to say everything that needs saying by saying nothing. Hold on to your social graces if you try speaking to someone who is already arguing internally with the emerging demon voices of what they now must suddenly accept is an absurdly abbreviated lifetime.

When she finally spoke of her lifeless hubby out loud, it was in the present tense as she looked at the rumpled cloth in her hand:

"He likes these socks."

This method of coping and dispensation is not in the survival books, but it is as non-stop and understated as water.

For the record: grief is private mourning, and mourning is public grieving. If you've never had to feel or display the difference, stick around long enough to outlive someone you love.

Then, just like that -- in more time than it takes to attach a word to a feeling, but less time to say so in this sentence -- you're alive and they aren't. Sometimes it does not come as a thief in the night.

Sometimes it's the home-baked goods table at everyone's favorite charity bazaar at high noon.

I hope that one of those vice versas will be easier.

Still, she'd always hated those socks, and people have gone crazy and drowned in their own fluids over much less. Cats have.

I will.

PAUL NEWMAN'S DOG'S AT 4:23

Without getting into the messy-ness of it, I can tell you that he once stole a chew toy belonging to a dog owned by Paul Newman.

Paul Newman's dog's chew toy.

Well, alright ... I can see right now that you're ready for a mess, so this time you won't mind a few more details:

Life is full of surprises, which was why he was always surprised that his wasn't.

As the night watchman at a landmark North Country tavern, he made his rounds every night on foot, checking-in at the stations throughout the main building and its outlying historic cottages. No surprises there.

He carried a Watchman's Clock: a heavy, round device encased in black leather. It had a clock face, a keyhole, and a thick leather shoulder strap that always left chafe marks below one side of his neck. He didn't have to carry it that way so that it did, but he felt that he had to so it would. This is why there'll never be a shortage of lonely men willing to perform this job, a job that really is, let's face it, a means of letting their bosses know where they were at night, not where the insecurity was.

Most of everything that's right and everything that's wrong with America can be found in that dandy little philosophy.

At every stop, he inserted that station's key into the clock's keyhole and turned it. This left a time-stamp on the clock's interior ticker tape, confirming that at 2:10 a.m. he'd been at the end of the top floor hallway, outside the Franklin Pierce Suite, e.g.

Franklin Pierce's Suite's ghost didn't mind. It was drunk and off conspiring with secessionists, and sometimes they were all joined by the ghost of Ethan Allen. It had a room across the hall and hadn't been sober since 1932, when the Republic of Vermont began turning a Revolutionary War hero's adventures into bedroom furniture.

Or, at 3:13 a.m., the clock's tape showed that the night watchman had arrived in the foyer housing the Rudyard Kipling Fountain. Rudyard Kipling vacationed at the tavern in 1892, and just ahead of his visit, the owners moved an outdoor fountain inside and named it after him, thinking that it would be good for business and a big hit with Rudyard Kipling. Tavern keepers thought and still think like this, thanks to George Washington.

The Rudyard Kipling Fountain.

Rudyard Kipling's liquids flowed here.

They made a little ceremony out of it when he arrived, but Rudyard Kipling didn't attend. He was flattered, but was busy writing anywhere else but there. As it happened, the anywhere else was on the tavern's second floor's Room 214, in what would later become the Robert Frost Room.

It was a working vacation.

At that time in time, Robert Frost was busy graduating ahead of his class from Lawrence High School, so Rudyard Kipling avoided the fountain ceremony by secreting himself in what was still Room 214. You don't get a room named after you for graduating early from Lawrence High School. That dubious honor is reserved for long-lived (but with a decent interval of long-dead) poets.

Years later, when the Kipling craze died down and no one seemed to care that their accommodations included a bonus proximity to the Rudyard Kipling Fountain, the owners had a plaque made to go with it:

The Rudyard Kipling Fountain plaque read:

Rudyard Kipling used this site
as a favorite writing retreat
during an extended visit here in 1892.

It wasn't true, but even though plaques are known for being full of shit, they're effective. Anything that rings permanent in this temporary world, shit-filled or not, is worth selling and reselling, if only for the simple care and comfort of our souls.

After that, business boomed, and thanks to word of mouth, a century of literary reawakenings and colorful brochures that included plaque pictures later, the tavern's guests began making reservations, sometimes a year in advance, for rooms in the building with the Rudyard Kipling Fountain.

There's your tip, if nothing else works for you here: Stay dead or in a state of debauchery long enough, especially in literature, and you'll get picked up by another crop of revisionists.

When the tourists arrived, they fell prey to the magical thinking that always goes along with such claims of secondhand greatness. They threw coins into the water, making solemn wishes that would or wouldn't be granted for reasons other than Rudyard Kipling, dead or alive.

They sat and dipped their feet, and some of them even sipped from the Rudyard Kipling Fountain, believing that remnants of Rudyard Kipling's body's DNA would wash off inside them.

They wouldn't, of course, because it's almost certain that Kipling never waded in, drank from, or even went near the thing. He had a pathological fear of water, which is why it appeared as a principal player in many of his works. But, it didn't give the honeymooning Kipling readers an excuse for never becoming great writers, and that was enough.

We'll have to wonder if the Rudyard Kipling Fountain was a distant but pivotal inspiration for, say, *The Crab That Played With The Sea*, or *How The Whale Got His Throat*, or *Captains Courageous*. I'd like to think so:

> *"… As the smooth-backed rollers passed*
> *to the southward, they hove the dory high*
> *and high into the mist, and dropped her*
> *in ugly, sucking, dimpled water …"*

Less lofty refrains have sprung from muse prompted by more celebrated perches, but it could've happened just that way on a dry sloping corner of the pre-Frostian, Joseph Rudyard Kipling's tavern's Room 214's desk.

Meanwhile, the kitchen & dining room staff stole the Rudyard Kipling Fountain coins and used them to buy booze.

The night watchman was big on talismans, not because he believed in them, but because he wanted to, so he attached that much importance to them, like half-heartedly praying with a stolen rosary missing a few beads.

The night watchman also liked kidding himself that he always knew what God was going to do next. Then, he'd step out of the way at the last second, dodging destiny and outwitting a Supreme Being.

It never really worked, of course, not because he believed it couldn't, but because he wanted it to, like the night he stole Paul Newman's dog's chew toy.

As he stood outside the Daniel Webster Cottage, reaching for that station's watch key at 4:23 a.m., he noticed a figure moving inside the kitchen.

It was Paul Newman.

Holy Jesus! Right there, a few feet away! Eddie Felson. Rocky Graziano. Hud Bannon. Hank Stamper. Brick Pollit. Butch Cassidy. The salad dressing guy. In the flesh!

Every winter, Paul Newman and Joanne Woodward rented the Daniel Webster Cottage. Daniel Webster's ghost couldn't have cared less. It was usually off on a bender with Ethan Allen, which always brought its own chair, the Green Mountain boys, who always came armed, Franklin Pierce, who always did most of the talking, and the sous chefs, who always drank most of the booze.

They'd invite the idea of the ghost of Robert Frost, but it would never show. It always took the less traveled road, got lost, and wound up back in Lawrence, Massachusetts, graduating high school two years early.

I'm sure you can see where Rod Serling or Alfred Hitchcock would've climbed over Stephen King for the rights to this story.

The Newmans spent their winter vacation riding around the snowbound village streets on Skidoos and insisting that no one bother them. They always made a big noisy show of insisting that they be left alone. The locals didn't mind. They made a big quiet show of leaving them alone.

The night watchman thought he'd again outwit God at that moment, but, as always, the Ol' Deity was on His game, because there was holyjesus Paul Newman standing at the inn's Daniel Webster's cottage's kitchen counter in his underwear, making a sandwich at 4:23 a.m.

Astonishing. This was the last thing the night watchman ever thought he'd see. This surreal scene was a pip, even for God.

Paul Newman made his own sandwiches? Unbelievable. If he were Paul Newman instead of a bitter, used-up ex-deputy sheriff working the night shift not because he wanted to but because he believed he had to, he'd have a personal sandwich maker: someone he paid to sit in the spare bedroom in the Daniel Webster Cottage at the ready, night or day, to jump up and make him a sandwich on demand.

Sure, the guy could fill-in as his combo snowmobile mechanic and dog handler, but his primary job would be to make him sandwiches.

"I'm hungry. Make me a sandwich," he'd yell to his snowmobile dog handler mechanic/sandwich servant without getting out of bed, if HE were Paul Newman.

The night watchman quickly moved from the shock of disillusionment to anger. Paul Newman shouldn't have to make his own sandwiches. He wouldn't, if he were him! His anger was beginning to cloud his reason.

At the very least, if HE'D been immortalized as Chance Wayne, he'd wake up Princess Kosmonopolis and insist that she whip him up a pastrami on rye.

Worst of all, standing there in the dimly lit kitchen at that hour, Paul Newman had the blanched, rickety-pickety legs of an ordinary old man. White tee shirt, white boxer shorts, and bit player gams.

Most unexpected. It would not do, and for the first time in his life the night watchman was really surprised, and it pushed him just out in front of what God had planned for his next move.

On the ground under the watch station box, a well-gnawed chew toy was tipped into the snow. It obviously belonged to Paul Newman's dog: the one that rode around town with Cool Hand Luke himself on his snowmobile. The dog barked constantly on those jaunts, insisting that the town's dogs ignore him, too.

The night watchman picked up the shredded hard rubber chew toy, jammed it into his pocket and walked away, abandoning the clock-in. Most unwatchman-like.

But, he was now overcome with an aging, ex-deputy sheriff's lifelong's great unexpectations, and was personally pissed off at Paul Newman for making his own sandwiches and for having such understudied legs. The act of stealing Paul Newman's dog's chew toy had finally just outplayed God's grand design. At that point, punching a clock had zero significance for him.

It fast became so insignificant that he didn't finish the rest of his rounds. What? The civic-minded man who wouldn't miss an appointed duty in his life even if he had to crawl along on bloody stumps? The man who once achieved local lawn enforcement infamy by flagging down the governor's car and handing him a speeding ticket while on foot patrol? (Even God had done a double take on that one.)

Instead, he went home, stripped down to his underwear, made himself a pastrami on rye and never went back to work. It was the angriest sandwich he'd ever made.

Do I need to tell you what an angry sandwich looks like? I didn't think so.

I also won't tell you where he did go after that or what he did to get there. You wouldn't believe it, but let's just say that it was a creative and messy enough finale to put a Creator out of the prognostication business.

A week later, a tavern guest masquerading as an aquaphobic Gunga Din, fished a night watchman's clock out of the Rudyard Kipling Fountain and brought it to the front desk.

Somewhere in America, Paul Newman's dog's chew toy still hasn't surfaced, but we know where it is.

Surprise.

AN ECHO OF GOD
AS WINTER FLOWER

Few subjects are as indelicate as this, but I'm pressed for time today, and with a title as compelling as the one up there, I have no choice but to get right to it:

She had hairy nipples.

Too hairy.

There. Now, I could try to salvage this and rescue you from your queasiness by changing the subject and instead write about, oh, the crushing humility you feel when you ask a very young girl to draw a picture of God, and she draws a simple, three-petaled solitary flower, gently breaking your heart.

That's another lovely story all by itself, but you need to hurry up and forget that tender blush for now, because it's a bitterfuckcold December morning, the furnace has quit, and I've suddenly been filled with the long dormant memory of an unheated loft apartment and a beautiful woman's unexpectedly hairy nipples.

In fact, I had the same reaction back then, when she pulled off her sweater, that I had this morning when I awoke to ice forming on the inside of my bedroom windows:

"Whoosh! It's going to be a long winter. TOO long. Maybe I can shorten it," I'd reacted.

I said it out loud today, alone.

Silently, back then, with her.

Silently, back then, with her.

EARLY RETIREMENT
BY THE NUMBERS

Yes, it was the same country road he'd traveled every day to work. Let's call him Leo. We'll call him Leo because his name wasn't Leo, (an inside rural joke) and considering his outcome, he deserves to at least have you take that away from here, and it's just the kind of outcome that you'd expect for a guy not named Leo.

"Hear what happened to Leo?"

"You mean that guy with that car?"

"Yeah. I'm not surprised. Sounds just like him."

Admit it: there are some fates you've seen play out in this life that simply fit, according to your idea of a good fit.

It was a longer drive than an alternate route he might have used, but Not Leo went that way because it didn't go "as the crow flies," as they say, and that's how his mind worked in general, and lately in particular.

Wandering. Full of detours and roundabouts.

The expression had never made sense to him, anyway, because he'd once seen a crow make an abrupt, aerial about-face while heading toward the top of a maple tree, opting instead for an oak branch WAY OVER THERE at the last second, flying first way out and way back and for no apparent reason. Imagine a swoop bluntly interrupted, as if the sky had suddenly turned cartoon, and with another dimension to it.

The granddaddy of all winged, bent horseshoe-shaped blasted zigzags, with the wind as shotgun. Now you've got it.

It made him feel good and a bit smug that he hadn't been the first one in history to write "as the crow flies." There were claims for its first authorship everywhere in history, from British merchant ship sailors to Pennsylvania piemakers, and it has sifted from one century into another like alphabet soup through panty hose.

Only historians are allowed to be off by a hundred years and a continent or two, but that's how we operate as descendees: when any profoundly simple but universal ditty catches on, we all want a piece of it.

Meanwhile, Not Leo suspected it was one guy all along (not his own inner devil Crow Fly Guy, but not far off) who first said it as an afterthought, probably under his breath on a crowded sidewalk while walking close enough to an unscrupulous writer who then ran off with it, published it eponymously and finally sold it to British seafarers who used it to find America and barter it away for some shoofly pie on their first Pennsylvania shore leave.

Panty hose was still far off in the future, and we'll have to save the history of alphabet soup for another time.

And, yes, the Keystone State has a seaside shoreline (an inside rural Pennsylvania joke).

But, what good was any ditty, and who cared how widely used it was, no matter the century, when your ship was sinking? Are you kidding? Long-waterbound sailors would take full bellies any day, and at least go down to the sea in shoo fly pies, well-fed.

Seamen have always been satisfied with simple pleasures.

Not Leo wished he'd had a movie camera when he'd seen his crow make nonsense out of that already extra-sensical saying. He wished he'd filmed the crow when it had inexplicably pulled up short of a head-on collision with a capricious flight plan and changed direction, looking very much like it was taking the long way 'round the barn.

There's our dilemma, and it might seem small compared to what happened to Not Leo, but if a crow can fly the long way 'round the barn, we'll have to be on guard for sidewalk stranger historian types looking for hot tag lines.

We might not, but Not Leo would've taken the movie and shown it to Crow Fly Guy, the guy who first came up with the saying:

"There. Now try being wise with something else. That one's bogus, buddy boy," he'd tell him.

Crow Fly Guy would try to weasel out of his highly overrated and widely touted contraband air measure:

"Okay, then how about using this instead: 'As the crow flies into an invisible and imaginary plate glass window in a fourth-dimensional cartoon sky.' Happy now?"

Yes, Not Leo would have been.

Some of the above is close to what psychiatrists call "flight of ideas." Not Leo would've liked that, if he'd cared about what psychiatrists thought. He didn't, but it's probably more important right now that you and I don't.

The road to work was familiar as usual, and Not Leo was having this conversation again with Crow Fly Guy in his mind as he drove along. Until now, little did you know that he'd had it many times before, and it had always ended with him mentally running the smart-ass aviarian pithyist off the road into one degree of calamity or another.

He'd traveled this road for so long, in both directions, that he knew everything about it, going to and coming back from work. Enroute, he knew where and when a bone-shaking spring frost heave turned into a summer asphalt dimple, and he'd driven accordingly.

Coming back, he knew just where and how fast he could hug the road's solid line in a winter corner because the defoliated thicket there gave him a clear view of oncoming traffic.

Going either way, all these seasons later, he knew just where and if he could coast, and just where and why he would brake. The road had given him everything he'd ever wanted in a wife, but had never found. He was a confirmed rules-of-the-road bachelor. No dead-end marital bliss for our boy Not Leo.

He'd come and gone to and from work on this road for … how many miles now? He could've told you the exact number if he'd added them up, but assigning a finite label to anything forever removed its illusion of forever-ness, and he liked the prospect of infinity in his life, especially on this morning, his last day on the job.

This morning, if you had ironclad proof that infinity had mile markers and a destination, Not Leo would tell you just where you could stuff your mile markers and your destination.

Now add that he'd just run Crow Fly Guy off the road again, but this time hadn't waited around to see if he'd survived the crash. The last thing he saw was Crow Fly Guy's car smashing into an above ground pool, and a torrent of water rushing over the hood.

It was a spectacular fancy. Maybe his best ever.

Sometimes, when he was feeling merciful, he had Crow Fly Guy flying off a cliff and dying immediately on impact, or just tearing up a few guardrails after blowing a tire, sparing him but destroying his car. That was his favorite, because Crow Fly guy always went pale with terror and had to thumb home.

But, this time, Not Leo wanted his imaginary scapegoat to drown slowly in a swimming pool windshield tsunami, trapped in his seatbelt. Good. The pretentious prick wouldn't be trying to pass himself off as an expert in bird flight shortcuts anymore.

After all, weren't there enough finite things in life? A billion years ago, weren't the same Elemental ingredients that were now his bumpers, his very car, once parked underneath a glacier somewhere? And, wasn't his realtor brother-in-law always telling him: "Well, they aren't making any more land," then trying to sell him some? But, the proposal that anyone could "own" land only made sense to him if he'd been born immortal.

Otherwise, for all of us, eventually it's the one-way road of no return, and the land always comes back to own our lives like a bum uncle owns our hide-a-bed.

"If you show me how to pack two hundred acres in a hearse," Not Leo would tell his brother-in-law, "then maybe we'll talk."

That would shut him up for a month or two, but he'd always come around again trying to convince Not Leo that if only he'd buy some land from him, he'd live forever.

Not Not Leo.

So, how many miles was this?

345,461? 406,923? 501,299?

More? Less? Any or none of the above? He could figure it out, but he wouldn't.

Now there's a fascinating thought: Did he not know all the things in his life that he could figure out but wouldn't, and know all the things he would figure out but couldn't?

He'd be happy if the two were self-canceling, so he decided to make that number zero. There. No more mysteries. Mysteries are only mysterious if we labor to unravel them. Mysteries denied can't trouble us.

Not Leo, along with us, didn't know how many stars were in the cosmos. Even the expert star-counters among us don't know. He'd never lost any sleep over it, and let's agree that we won't, either. There's not enough time in this life for star-counting.

There's hardly enough time to get to the bank.

All Not Leo could really be sure of was that this was his last trip to and from work, and the final tally was best kept in the Invisible Hall of Statistics where none of us are allowed admittance. Not in this existence, anyway.

Somewhere, the Curator of the IHS knew this number, along with the countless other minutiae of his life, like how many gallons of fluid had passed through and out of him, or how many feet of kite string had gotten away from him in his boyhood, or how many times how many women in his life hadn't given him a second glance.

Yes, somewhere those numbers were finite, but not for Not Leo, and that's how he wanted it.

This is not what Not Leo was thinking as he was penultimately killing Crow Fly Guy in his mind and heading to his last day on the job.

Instead, his imagining eyes were looking for a fun ironic twist and inserting his land-grubbing brother-in-law in the back, behind Crow Fly Guy's flooding passenger seat for good measure, and that distraction took his real eyes off the road just long enough to prompt this report from the Curator:

Days of work missed in 6,211 days: One.
Number of miles traveled on last day of work: 15.4.
Weight of the moose: 1, 421 pounds.
Direction taken by moose stepping into the road:

Not as the crow flew.

OH NO, YOKO, NOT FIFTY-FIFTY

"Just turn left at Greenland."
--John Lennon

We slip by death every day.

Like John signing that autograph.

Right here, you have my permission to remember that champion of the boorish characters in your lives, the one back then with the reluctant girlfriend no one ever invited but who always found his way to the pot party. He'd bust in with Miss Reluctant and lay lines like these on anyone who'd listen:

"Yeah, and what if yesterday, some dude in Canada slipped on his front steps, holding up his stateside call to his sister in Iowa City long enough for her to miss a dentist appointment?

"So, the dentist left work early and backed over a kid on a bike an hour before he should have been there. And the kid is my aunt's neighbor's kid. She cancels her trip back East so she can babysit this neighbor's other kids while he's in intensive care.

"Now, she and my uncle don't show up this weekend, Michelle and I go out tonight to the pizza place instead, run into Roachclip, here, and we follow him to this party. We've now changed the fates of everyone here because some Canuck fell down some stairs. Far out, man."

This same storyteller believed the material world formed as he approached it, solidified as he passed through it, and disintegrated as he left it. This brought on some serious scrapping with Miss Reluctant, a woman unappreciative of being considered an existential piece of ass.

He also proposed that "the enfuckintire universe could be a speck on a speck on a hair of a mayfly's wingtip," and any minute now we could slide into froglong oblivion.

This is the same guy now selling shitbox stereos within the clearly measurable confines of an interdenominational appliance store.

The point is: John Lennon might have perished for the lack of a Northern non-skid doormat.

Have a look at the man.

The man who, because of a goofy sequence of randomings, might rub you out with a gun or a knife or an innocent flicker of hesitation as he turns his VW on the parkway, and all because that morning, someone's toothache had to wait another day in Canada and some chick loath to go out just had to have pizza to stay in.

Have a good look today.

Right.

There.

DNIHEB UOY.

That could be him or his transcendental agent, standing on your banana peel, waiting to pay his tax bill.

Should you speak to him and save your life? Wait. Not so fast. If you do say something, tomorrow you too could be dead as pizza. Whichever you choose, try to leave me out of the equation.

I'll give both of us even odds, either way.

FISH PUNS IN THE FUTURE
OF PRESENTS PAST

The Bag Lady arrives at the funeral on foot.

She is wearing comfortable multi-season shoes and a drab, buttoned-up overcoat uniquely suited to her amorphous frame, giving the impression of a human form consisting entirely of head, hands and feet.

If clothes make the woman, we must linger on this for a moment:

No other person in the world could possibly fit into this coat. When she dies, the coat goes with her. We're talking a perfect fit that goes beyond the kind you get with any coat if you wear it long enough.

This is a symbiotic relationship with a garment.

A millennium from now, archeologists will take diggings of this astounding article of outerwear, when it is found fossilized alongside what look like knitting needles. They won't know what they are, because the last sheep would have fallen victim to natural selection in the year 2412, more than 200 years before the last museum housing a genus Ovis carcass was pulverized in the Great Warticulture of 2625.

Still, some overzealous young historian might record: *"The Most Significant Discovery Of A Sepulchral Raiment Since The Shroud Of Turin."*

Or, Archaeological Digest might proclaim: *"Proof That Funeral Bag Ladies Were Not Mythical Creatures."*

Even the Interplanetary Enquirer might get into the act, with: *"Ancient Lady Of Death Coat Found On Jupiter."*

Back at the funeral, Bag Lady enters lugging a wooden-handled carpetbag. It is overstuffed with knitting needles, and anchors of yarn trail out of it as she moves through the gathering of mourners. She looks like an overcoat-boat trolling for carpet fish.

Slowly, she rows her way over to the family, letting out more line. The conversation is what we'd expect:

"Did you know the deceased well?" she asks. Behind her, a helpful mourner is reeling in the yarn and stuffing it back in the carpetbag.

"Yes. He was my father," says the young sitting man who looks like he's been assigned the job of family spokesperson. It is possible to tell this by the way he doesn't get up. Sometimes, how we don't move says it all.

Actually, most times that's the case.

"Oh, my, isn't that wonderful. Imagine that. Your father," she says.

"I'm sure he'd be pleased, knowing you were here," responds the motionless son, expertly static. "May I ask your name?"

She sighs heavily, dabs the mist from her eyes daintily, pinches his wrist twistingly, and ignores his question completely, then wanders off to comfort another bereaver, dropping more skein lures in her wake.

During the Service, she sits way in the back, sniffling, nodding, and knitting. A gaudy turtleneck sweater disguised as a baby blanket begins to emerge from the carpetbag.

The following month, the sit-still son will receive it in the mail.

After the Service, she collects the sweater/blanket, reloads the carpetbag, backs into and needle-harpoons the line of receivers, and makes her way through the crowd to the street, sighing, dabbing and twisting her way to the sidewalk. Decks awash in yarn, she puts about for the horizon.

Now, on to the old gentleman standing in the kitchen:

No one knows how he arrives at the wake. He wears a bow tie on a buttoned-down flannel shirt, and a timeless pair of bib overalls generically suited to his square frame, giving the impression of a human form consisting entirely of torso.

If clothes make the man, here is the finished product:

Every other man in the world could fit into these overalls. When he dies, these overalls will go to the thrift shop. We're talking an ageless, universal fit. One size fits all.

If they were ten years younger, man and overalls, they'd look the same.

A millennium from now, one archaeologist will ask another how he came by that pair of perfect overalls, just the thing for rooting around on your knees while taking radiographs of thousand-year-old overcoats.

Apparently, future archaeologists will take their work home with them on occasion.

Back in the kitchen, he moves through the gathering of mourners. He looks like the headless horseman in bricklayer's formal wear.

He courses his way over to sit-still son, laying a foundation of standard epitaphs with all the friends and relatives enroute. The conversation solves the day's mystery:

"My wife knew your father," he announces from somewhere in the space above his bow tie. Behind him, one cousin has convinced another to go get a tetanus shot for the only known instance of funereal knitting needle stabbing in history.

"Really? How?" sit-still son asks politely, his curiosity begging him to know whoinheck this old man is.

"She was at the Service this afternoon. Asked me if I'd drop by and pay my respects. Said she was sorry she couldn't be here, but she had to attend another funeral."

"Oh. Sorry to hear that."

"We appreciate that, son. Now, just remember: Don't go meeting your troubles halfway. Let 'em go the distance. Something just might happen to 'em before they get to you."

A month later, when the oversized, multicolored turtleneck sweater anonymously arrived in the mail, sit-still son thought it just the thing to take out the evening chill on a fishing trip.

For our purposes, it was just enough to prompt an unmoving heir to get going and look at life from a whole new angle.

THE NICE FIRST THOUGHT

It was a nice first thought, and it had just come into his head.

All of our arriving mentations are like that, first fitting us like the skins of balloons.

We float inside them, feeling luxurious. We also feel well-defined and trapped by them, but that's how the first rule of luxury, and the insides of balloons, work. Second rule? When the balloons break, it's back to the soup kitchens of second thoughts, bub.

Second thoughts will do, and do make do, mostly, but we'd never think of taking one to a formal affair.

He liked the nice first thought so much that he wanted to use it in his own humor writings. He would find a way, he thought. Another first.

As reader, you now have all the workings of an epic saga going for you. Just in what you know so far, you could, with just a dash of ingenuity, squeeze the life of an Isadora Duncan out of this and tell all of her inside-a-balloon life story in the time it takes to lurch between clutch and accelerator.

It was a nice first thought, but, on second thought, he decided to keep it to himself and make soup.

B. Elwin Sherman

SITTING AT HIS KEYBOARD,
THE APPROXIMATE POLE LAMP MEETS
AN EARTHQUAKE DANGLING PARTICIPLE

Smash!

PPPPPPPPPPPPPPPPPPPPPPPPPPPPPPPPPPPPPPPP
PPPPPPPPPPPPPPPPPPPPPPPPPPPPPPPPPPPPPPPP
PPPPPPPPPPPPPPPPPPPPPPPPPPPPPPPPPPPPPPPP
PPPPPPPPPPPPPPPPPPPPPPPPPPPPPPPPPPPPPPPP
PPPPPPPPPPPPPPPPPPPPPPPPPPPPPPPPPPPPPPPP
PPPPPPPPPPPPPPPPPPPPPPPPPPPPPPPPPPPPPPPP
PPPPPPPPPPPPPPPPPPPPPPPPPPW0[IG[0VPO,DF-][K-][

THE ENVELOPE

What happened?

It had an antagonist:

A middle-aged, balding bejeweled power broker with never proven but always suspected gangland ties, corrupting all characters within with lures of money, drugs and sex. A smattering of antagonist's helpers collected the money, dispensed the drugs and arranged the sex.

These same weasels also stole Mr. Big's money, altered the drugs and pimped on their own. Thus, it had the requisite background miniplots of backcrossing and doublestabbing weaving throughout.

It had a protagonist:

A dashing, former campus radical turned politically conservative, haunted by an Amerasian heir line, stalked by Mr. Big's weasels and seduced by Mr. Big's weaseltress. The weasels bungled the job repeatedly. She, of course, fell for our big lovable lunk and in turn turned turncoat on Mr. B. and confessed all to hero-san. She died in a hail of Mr. B.'s lead, but not before delivering a love child, courtesy of Mr. B.'s shady resources.

As treachery would have it, the Big Man was ruined at the hand our righteous Republican's avenging rage and killed himself by (well … he'd still been working on that, and had left it out of the outline).

A crippled college rival, a meddling janitor, an eyewitness cabbie and a pride of bribed detectives also made witting and unwitting appearances.

He'd sprinkled all this with dark humor, ancestral taboos, luscious scenery and compelling dialogue:

"Can you ever forgive me, Frank, for being such a fool?"

"Sure, baby. I'll forgive you. With this."

"Ooooh, Frank, I never dreamed it could be so---" for instance.

He'd mailed it fifty years ago.

Where the hell was it?

He'd sent return postage.

He was sure of it.

THE LITTLE WOMAN

Now, listen. I'm telling you this in my mind because you're long gone. At this late date, it will have to do.

It just never mattered.

Together, at the cupboards, if it was cleanser I wanted, I didn't have to bend over. If it was cereal you wanted, you didn't have to reach. It was the stuff that made up good comedy teams.

When we stood, your mouth rested on my chest, at a spot tall women ignored.

When we stretched out together, if you'd been taller, you'd have just had more leg slapping the air.

Who'd have cared?

Not me. You were short on legs.

I was long on you.

WHEN A PLUMBER MURDERS

The fat plumber sat on his seatless toilet.

The seat never had a chance against his weight. It had splintered and fallen away six months ago. When his cheating wife wasn't, he'd replaced it. Now that she was, he didn't anymore.

Now, he just plunked down on the scummy perimeter, not caring about the seat bolts spiking him in the buttocks.

In the tiny bathroom he sat on the broken toilet, leaning forward, hands in the sink. It was pitifully small, if one were to judge sink size by the bulk of body parts put there. The basin held his ten fingers, but five caught hot, five caught cold.

Unscrubbable rust stains from unstoppable drips mixed with the green streaks under the fixtures. The handles lay in the soapdish. Stripped of conventional turning power, they had to be manually applied, given considerable side- and then downward pressure to turn them on and off.

Toilet and sink, the whole thing was a disgrace for a plumber, but he was way beyond shame. That had swiftly moved in and just as swiftly moved out when his pipefitting pride went to hell, and that had happened when he'd come home early that time and heard them together in the bathroom.

He'd left and come back later after driving around aimlessly in his plumbing truck for the million years of torture that anyone in that mindset can pack into four hours, then begun his forever never caring again about leaks. Along with the sounds of sexplay he'd heard in there, the water had been running. He'd tried to get that out of his mind.

Impossible for a plumber, and an especially fruitless pursuit for a heartsick-crazy turning slowly murderous one.

Shortly after that, she'd moved out, and he was left with a life distilled down to hating the sound of water and the sight of a pipe.

The stopper wouldn't recess snugly, (another plumbing dishonor) so a rag had to be wedged in to hold the water. He'd been using a raggedy pair of her traitorous panties for six seatless months.

The sink was clogged.

He jiggled the stopper.

The sink was clogged.

He tugged on the stopper, measuredly, as if defusing a bomb.

But, when he raised it from the drain----

He found her tampon earring string and hairpin and painted toenail clippings and toothpaste cap snarled in a gloopglop of condom whiskersnot that looked like it came from the scalp of Medusa.

(Okay, as you've been expecting, you may now Insert travel time of a fat man going from bathroom to pipe wrench to ex-wife's boyfriend's house.)

LAUREN BACALL ON CAMELBACK

She had eyes that knew the first and last great source of all suffering love: having lived and then living someone else's notion of who she was.

She knew he knew it.

To stay longer would've clinched it, and dried up any chance of ever using her last defenses.

To be lonely alone or lonely with him?

This was her choice, over the isolation of a companion contemptuous of his definition of her.

She chose instead to move across sand in search of a desert flower, rather than be left rooted and blooming in a barren land.

Bogart, that night, traded guns for water.

THE LOST CRUCIFIXIONS

I don't know what they're called these days.

Let's just say that they were men living in a halfway house who were incapable of ever living independently in a full house. Not a threat to society, but forever needing cognition-competent adult supervisors for the rest of our lives.

Yes. I meant *our* up there. We're the nervous ones.

A healthcare professional might call such men "easily led."

I once heard a nurse say that about one of her confused elderly patients: "He's easily led." That made me sad. Sad enough to stop dating her. Right then I knew that she was someone I didn't want to grow old with. I never wanted to be easily led. I preferred being "a tough act to follow."

Too bad, because she had one great body. She's probably now using what's left of it to easily lead what's left of her old man around somewhere, the poor sonovabitch.

Again, these halfway men were not willfully dangerous; they'd committed no crimes against humanity. They were just men who, through accident of birth or industrial mishap or who'd developed unknown organic hijinks later in life, could never fully separate reality from the perception of reality.

You know. Not people like us.

If you're suddenly feeling less safe, be at your ease and pay more attention. I said they weren't dangerous. You have more to worry about from people who can fully separate reality from the perception of reality, and often do.

You know. People like us.

One fine hot summer day, the undangerous men were collected by their overseer and taken to a pauper's cemetery: a closed burying ground containing former men like them, interred there in a time when such live men were housed in state-run institutions for the half unreality-based.

The institutions were sprawling complexes of big brick blocks with screened-in windows, all connected by tunnels. Lots of both-halves reality was committed there by people like us. That's why they were closed.

Of course, there's no such thing as a closed cemetery, unless you remove its tenants. In this way, an empty cemetery is not like an empty apartment house.

In the latter, you have an empty apartment house. In the former, you have dirt. You could put a sewage treatment plant on the site of an empty cemetery. Dirt is very accommodating that way. Try doing that in an empty apartment house. Imagine the problem just with the stairwells alone.

Official state records listed the cemetery as "inactive."

Odd, because a department of state is not known for having a sense of humor.

On this day, the tribe of half-displaced men was charged with tending the grounds of the formerly closed, officially inactive, but still occupied cemetery. For the older of these men, many of their former cohorts and relatives from the old days were there, waiting out eternity beneath simple white wooden crosses.

These cemetery residents were through not wondering about what is real and what they thought was real. Now, they knew. There's not much, however, that any enlightened soul can do to mess with you after its body has been deactivated. I told you not to worry.

The crosses had small metal disks on them. They were engraved, but not with names or dates.

Instead, Harrison Buckerton was there, under "C-424-D."

Alberto Miniff was over there, under "D-662-E."

Samuel Mattario was way over there, under "U-416-V."

All former tunnel-visionaries, now lastly reduced to the same letter-number identities as us. They're now just more accepting of it.

The half-brained men arrived with rakes and other implements of lawn-tending and were instructed by their caretaker to tidy up the place. Up until then, perpetual cemetery care had been performed by a fully-brained sub-contractor for the state. He'd lost the job when it was discovered that instead of weeding and raking, he'd spent the money on a trip to Disneyland.

Even the state officials couldn't find the humor in it, and I did tell you that we had to worry about people like that.

They replaced his sub-contract with the halfway house one. A harmless task for a harmless crew, or so thought the unusually good-humored state employees, and for a fraction of what they had allocated for a three-week junket to Main Street U.S.A.

"What could go wrong?" one of them might have asked, if atypically amiable state officials weren't always so preoccupied with what couldn't.

The local community was satisfied, because the men were off working instead of hanging around town making everyone uneasy (despite the assurances I've given you) by spending their time loitering above ground and scaring the children.

One problem: The overseer for the new lawn care crew was cut from the same recreational cloth as Disney-man. He'd dropped off his half-witless charges, left them alone to do the job and gone off to find the cold beer counterpart of Mickey's Toontown.

When he returned, he found that the men had done their assigned job very well. Too well. Way beyond the maximum efficiency realm of half-perceived reality kind of well.

Seems that Thad Buckerton, the half-wayward half-brother to C-424-D, had been inspired to lead his fellows in the elegantly simple method of inactive cemetery maintenance -- by uprooting the crosses and tossing them all together.

There they were, heaped up in a giant pile in the center of the grounds like a pickup-stick memorial to the human lost and found. There wasn't a weed in sight, and all the halfway house men were standing in a circle around the pile, smiling.

But, instead of panicking, and because alcohol is often the source of creative thinking, he told the men to just put back the crosses and pack up their tools.

They did.

He also congratulated them on the fine job.

This made them smile even more. He didn't need a reason to smile. He was drunk.

They returned the crosses in no particular order, shoving the crosses back into the ground sideways, leaving the wrong graves marked with their wrong single vertical stakes sticking up and transforming the place into a ringer for a vampire graveyard. That mattered about as much as the willy-nilly rearrangement.

It's now a near geo-mathematical certainty that Alberto Miniff and Samuel Mattario and Harrison Buckerton have forever switched their former earthly job descriptions.

I think Christ would be okay with that.

I am. I am. I am.

THE SLAPSTICK LINGERIE REDEMPTION

See her and him.

See her love him.

See her forgive him and laugh until she cried, even after he'd ruined their special wedding anniversary supper by coming home excuselessly late, leaping into their bedroom and unapologetically announcing, "Hide your daughters! I've got a bulletin in my britches!"

There were knots in his shoelaces, so he yanked off his shoes and flung them into a lamp without picking the damned little nodules out of themselves.

Raked off his socks without turning them outside-in afterward and rolling them into neat little crescent roll shapes like he always did.

Loosened his tie just enough to flip it over his head, the four-in-hand still an integral quartet.

Seized his shirt at the chest and Supermanned the buttons onto the carpet.

Snapped his belt around his waist hole-end first.

Ripped the zipperteeth to the crotch and back up his ass to the severed beltloops.

Shredded his briefs to the waistband.

Stood there -- peeled, panting and proudly penile -- looking for all the world like an x-rated outtake of a Three Stooges bombblast and a man who'd just try to lift himself off the floor by lifting himself off the floor.

But, even after this performance, he still took the time to kiss her everywhere with feathery fierceness, caress her anywhere with gentle, teasing traces, and lick her right there past all the lollipop candy on his way to the creamy center, waiting until SHE was ready for HIM.

This is why she loved him.

This is also why the idea of having to forgive him for splinting together the patio table umbrella pole with her favorite bra never entered her mind again.

ADELE HUGO A MINUTE LATER

Father believed that revolution was progress.
He said that philosophy was the microscope of thought.
He said that social prosperity made a happy man.

He also said that a woman was the devil.

There I go, Hugo.

THE UPPER MIDDLE-INCOME IN-LAWS ARE AVOIDED AT THE BARBEQUE

"Cost us a bundle," they would have said, had anyone asked.

"Cost us a bundle," they said, when no one did.

THE ICE AGE

One afternoon long ago, I was called to go and defrost the old people's icebox.

"Can you come over? Everything's stuck in there," he'd said, in an old voice made old by one too many real & imagined emergencies.

"Yes, certainly, I'll be right over," I'd replied, trying to sound accommodating while hiding my dread. I'd been to the old couple's home many times before to help them with this or that little job, but the calls had become frequent and were getting frequenter, probably because I was good at not letting on that I knew they were crazy and getting crazier.

When you start engaging the characters and circumstances in someone else's hallucinations, you've become their enabler.

What's that mean? I remember once being roughly awakened one night by the woman lying next to me. "GET UP! KILL THAT SPIDER!" she yelled. So, I did, and there I was, smacking my palms against a solid wall trying to kill the spider in her dream.

She was right, with the pesky arachnid being prompted by a vision in her sleeping dream and not a waking one, but I hated bugs, too, and I felt righter.

Bye-bye, spiderwoman.

Or, during one summer college semester break, I attended an old homebound man who needed help with his activities of daily living: washing, dressing, eating, and demanding that I shoo away the "blue angel" at the kitchen table.

"Shoo!" I said, before he'd let me sit him down for breakfast.

Bye-bye, angel of death. See you in my old age.

Meanwhile, now back and beyond the latter, I'm remembering an old icebox: the kind of freezer where the playmates in their hearts shoved mortar into their bloodstreams like bleach.

They'd had the same chunk of ice in there for sixty-seven years, and they were starving.

"When can you come?" he asked, already forgetting what I'd said.

"I'll be right over," I repeated, but I could hear the cold air from there. It sounded like a snowstorm at the equator.

Of course, they had cupboards full of food, but the bulging freezer had finally trumped all their other options of feeding themselves. To be fair, I suppose, young or old, you could make the case that a freezer on the fritz was a real emergency, if an advancing kitchen glacier made of fiction is your idea of a non-fictional crisis.

I asked them once, on a day I'd been summoned to find the source of a squeak in their bed, just how they'd managed to stay together so long.

"Never leave the door open," she'd said.

"Always keep the door shut," he'd said.

Normally, I'm pretty quick to see how life's metaphors will later become the lives themselves, but I'd missed that one. I was still young. It was a distinction that later became clear to me, when I'd failed to shut my (freezer) door. The resulting meltdown generated monthly power payments to a weekend icechip off the old block.

Not long before the big freeze, she sat on a park bench. Up came two kids, full of whoops, capguns and cowboy wisecracks. They shot CAPBANG and she CAPBANG hit the turf, clutching her heart. You got me, pardners, oh you got me. They beat it, bug-eyed scared little screaming shitless old lady-killers.

She smiled, pained but pleased. It was worth it but still hard to dammit get up.

By himself, he sat on a park bench. Up came a popcorn prowling pigeon. He pressed one nostril tight with a knuckle and took aim. Sixty-seven years of nasal warfare caught the feathered rookie square in the bird's-eye.

Together, they sat in their car, a mobile reflection of their increasing inability to thaw. Polished hubcaps. Even a polished antenna, topped with one of those fluorescent-painted Styrofoam parking lot signal buoy balls. All the doors doored and belts belted with the precision and quiet of rolling marbles.

Everything ached from infernal indibustion. Nothing Richard Petty couldn't cure.

But, now they were a couple of foregone infirmities, forgetting they had free will and there it was: the metaphors had won, like a comet duet.

If I didn't help them, they'd both likely slip and impale themselves on icepicks.

I didn't fix the icebox. It had won, too. When I arrived, it had completely consumed their house like a child's mind is consumed by a monster movie. They were outside in the garden, stuck fast in that last space left between an open and shut door, hardly a space at all.

A sliver of contemplation wouldn't have had wiggle room left over.

Instead, I called the family iceman and we took the old couple to the old icebox owner junkyard. They fit right in. The place was full of old icebox owners, all empty, some on their backs, some propped up.

All with their doors removed.

SPRING CLEANING, TOO LATE

If she'd been underneath there, if that only could have been her who appeared, waving her hand in the slow pendulum of spent love, if he only could've been with her outside his memory, even from there, then those sinking shreds in his center would have only been completely unbearable.

But, it wasn't her.

And, he was almost standing it.

It was an empty wall, as he'd known it was going to be, blotted by the box-whiteness of a long-hanging picture frame removed.

To Hell with spring cleaning.

It was fall, anyway.

PRE-HISTORIC MURPHY'S LAW

"Never trust a man with a vertical bed,"
is what fathers should say to daughters.

It's the same thing that sent the dinosaurs packing.

DISCOVERY PARADE FOR DUMMIES

A gazebo sits here at the water's edge, where drum & tuba bands play in the hot dusks of well-touristed summers.

The musicians are local amateur mainstays, some older than the traditional boom-bang marching tunes.

Always the straying semi-tone or errant upbeat.

But, if not for these exiled replays, my recollections of us would lie in the corner of a dusty attic like tossed ventriloquist dolls.

Across the lake in hazy affirmation, the mountains throw their voices.

Howee!

I can still step to the strains of uncomposed love marches without moving my legs.

SUPERBOY'S FALLEN BRANCHES

When I was a city boy I wished for things.

INVISIBILITY: I could ride the buses without transfers, always sit in the balconies, de-cap traffic cops, and watch everyone act in the privacies of their own mirrors, they thought.

Logistics was the problem.

Would food disappear once in my mouth?

Would I be the dreaming kind of invisible?   God-like, formless, untouchable, no bodily perimeter, yet still able to transmit and receive. Maintaining my quinsensibilities, even in the cast of my ultimate camouflage.

Or, if someone sat on me on the subway. Would they sit on me or through me?

What if I fell through a manhole or caught a stray bank heist bullet? Pain? Blood? Visible blood? Would I die?

Could I shoplift? A chest-high TV set bobbing across the intersection by itself would attract attention. And, if I could pick up a TV set and it did disappear, would it reappear when I set it down?

103

You can see the difficulties. I moved on.

To INVINCIBILITY: A force field, I figured, about eighteen inches away from my body all around, would do it. Then, on to the White House.

"I'd like to see the President."

"Sorry, kid. He's busy with the King of Megalomania."

"He can wait. I'm going in."

"Hey! Get back here!"

And, past the gate I'd go. All kinds of uniformed and plain-suited men would try to grab me, of course. They'd jump on my force field unharmed (I wouldn't be out for blood) but could not penetrate it or alter its direction. I'd walk in. They'd hold on. By the time I reached the Oval Office I'd be littered with hysterical agents and soldiers, all hanging on my horrible aura. I'd move through the door and squeegee them off. They'd lie there. Helpless.

"That's all right, boys. Let him in. He's obviously a boy who won't take no for an answer."

"Thank you, sir," I'd say. "Now, I have one demand."

"Name it," he'd say.

"Make me a grown-up," I'd demand.

"I'd like to, but I have to call your parents first," he'd say.

Everyone in the room laughed except the King of Megalomania, who suddenly had serious doubts about getting his foreign aid.

I moved on to exhaust the other possibilities that could stem from possessing such absolute power, even inserting a Kryptonian-style weakness to spice it up. It wasn't long before I realized that I could always never be beaten or always choose my own defeat. I lost interest.

I was led, as are the rest of us, to the final wistful wish:

INVALUABILITY:

Yes, if not for you, dear boy, those two toddlers would have certainly drowned in that vat of chocolate at the chocolate factory.

Their bodies would have been sucked down into the chocolate filtration stations, clogging the x-tillion dollar chocolate pipelines, costing the city untold more tillions in labor and chocolate replacement costs, and backing up countless sinks, tubs and toilets.

Not to mention the destruction and chaos created when the unshaven, foul-smelling, constipated voters then took to dumping their waste in the streets, causing widespread plague, pollution, chocolate riots and an Election Day upset.

You have, young man, quite likely saved my political career and the North American continent---nay, I say the world itself---from certain Armageddon.

Invisible.

Invincible.

Invaluable.

What I got was invalidated.

Now, as a country boy on the other end of life, I just wish I could wave my hand and change all their oil wells into toilets. Then just watch them try and raise the price per barrel. Ha!

But, also then, I suppose ….

I'd need a shit-powered chainsaw.

B. Elwin Sherman

THE OGDEN NASH SCHOOL OF TAXIDERMY

Her name was Sophie.
Our love's a trophie.

LUNAR FATHER'S DAY DINNER

Let's reduce the day to microbiology on the moon.

He had.

Heartache can do that to you, if you're not careful. An aching heart can turn itself into space travel if it finds the right launch pad.

His had.

He was being so-recognized and defined by the day because he once injected fluid into another human being, resulting in another human being.

No trick to that, and not his purpose or motivation at the time for doing it.

Fluid turned to solid: a solid whose main component was fluid.

And now, he's an estranged chemical engineer turned astronaut with another God-damned tie.

Even so, when the earth came into view, he wore the tie over his spacesuit.

It's lonely on the dark side of the moon. It's hard to breathe and the food is all unseasoned.

HISTORY OF THE EARLY
20ᵀᴴ CENTURY GRAND HOTEL FIRES

He wished he hadn't found the book.

He had enough to think about lately, wishing he hadn't lived this long, without letting seductive minutiae clutter up the place.

But wait, if he'd been looking for one, which he hadn't been, the book was as good a reason as any for putting suicide on the back burner.

The book and his life had long since been in the public domain, so he didn't have to feel guilty about taking a little more from either without permission.

The book looked like he felt, anyway, so what the hell. Any kinship in a storm.

Foxed and dog-eared pages, faded gilt lettering on the cover, torn-out frontispiece, scraped boards, dented spine, and any bookseller would've called it "uniformly age-toned." Man and book, a perfect match.

Inside?   An unforced march through another century's domestic jungle of now obsolete "chores, maladies, concoctions and cures."

Where did they go when their cues were silenced?   He was trying not to trouble himself with questions like that, so he began reading.

Here was the then all-consuming consumer guide to good health, long life and home management, packed with painstakingly composed protocols for bygone busy work.

Here was a seriocomic hymnal sung by a ghostly chorale. Here in his hands was lilac water, featherbed pillows, flatirons, corsets, bric-a-brac, whitewash, straw braids, tinware, Smyrna rugs, ice harvests, typhoid fever, consumption and arsenic soap.

Here was the world he'd wanted to die in, if only someone had asked him.

Did anyone still serve Continental Pudding or Twelve O'clock Pie or Oklahoma Rocks?   Of course not.   Continents, clocks and statehoods had all been replaced with artificial sweeteners, mechanical hands and cement.

Then, his eyes fell on a quote that put the misery back in his joy where it belonged:

"Have nothing in your house that you do not know to be useful or believe to be beautiful."

He cried a little, then took the book and went outside.

His ancestors all crowded around him under the tree. Men in stiff paper collars and straw boaters. Women in shirtwaist blouses, net gloves, long dresses and sporting human hair earrings. Boys and girls in knickerbockers, sailor suits, ostrich feathers and embroidered hems.

Now he was in the right mood, and he found himself reading aloud.

He read about how to whiten an unpainted wood floor by sprinkling white sand on it and leaving it there. Then, as the family walked to and fro, the traffic would scour the floorboards to a snowy whiteness.

He read about curing baldness by washing the head with Jamaican rum.

He read about dyeing the hair, (for the rum rubbers) "regarded by all intelligent persons as an unmistakable mark of vulgarity." One of his materfamilias blushed and hid behind her parasol.

He looked around. No other vulgar women in his matriarchal line-up, not until his photographer's modeling mother's sister came along and turned his 1957 family tree into a pinned-up pulp of petrified wood, sans parasol and most everything else.

He read about how to clear a foreign body from an airway by having the rescuer attach a bit of sponge to a whalebone and "shove it boldly down the throat." Now, even his six-year old grandfather stopped sucking on a clay marble and paid attention. His five-year old grandmother held her Babyland Rag Doll a little closer.

He read about how smeared-on horseradish would remove freckles, how to rid your house of rats by painting them with a phosphoric mixture, how any animal showing signs of rabies should be cauterized with a hot iron, how swallowing dissolved charcoal would cure bad breath, and how "no one should ever neglect the monthly shampoo."

He also read about how floors should be washed with gasoline and flannel, and how they should ventilated thoroughly "before admitting a light."

Damn. How he hated the 21st Century.

THE FUNNY LOVE LETTER
For J.W.

Was it too much to ask, at the end of his life, to write one original thing?

Yes, yes, yes, anyone could make the case -- and writers always do, in most unoriginal ways -- that all their work is original.

True enough, but all writing is original the way every wave breaking on the beach is original.

Each one different. Just like the indistinguishable collisions in the one before it. He'd been sitting there all afternoon, and at wave #156, he'd tried to recall wave #42.

Sorry. Wave #157 put the kibosh on that. And now, look. #158? Ditto.

#159. #160. #161 ....

No, no, no, that would not do. He wanted to write something (a simple sentence would suffice) that he KNEW had never been written and would never be written.

He wanted to write that one and only wave that, instead of amateurishly breaking on the beach like the ones before and after it, would turn to oatmeal, morph into cotton candy, harden into the shape of a Hoosier cabinet and spit out rainbow flour.

That sentence right there might just do it, he thought, if he hadn't had a friend, he remembered, who'd once told him that that's exactly what he'd seen after eating psilocybin mushrooms, except that in his version, the Hoosier cabinet had been topped with a melting halo and had a big toothy chicken on top of it. No, no, NO!

One must think past the endless permutations found in psychotropic muse, and in dreams, and in dreams of dreams, if one is to generate the last archetype.

He wanted to write a wave with only one ocean, an ocean that disappeared after offering up that one and only wave. An ocean that immediately became a field of roses.

Turns out, what he wanted to write was her.

But, just to be safe, he'd add a smiling chicken.

TWO POINT TWO

She was there at dusk, wrapped in a mauve wet suit like a plum, lightly drawing her fingers across her abdomen, and dipping a tentative toe in a twirling tidepool. She looked at him, but he was hiding in the open. She turned away. Women know exactly how much time to allot for such men.

Men paying more attention to musing a silly alliteration than they are to them.

Two point two seconds.

He was suddenly reduced to carrying pencil and pad for much the same reason that a boy who never has used a condom, and wouldn't know how to if he did, carries one anyway.

Before he knew it, and even after failing the 2.2 test, he found himself squeaking along haltingly through the hot sand and stopping when he was standing beside her. The pad and pencil slipped from his hand and plopped into her toe-bath. She stirred them in. He didn't have a clue what to say.

"Hello, Marilyn. My name is Arthur Miller," he said, the clue finding him. Contrived and conquered and condomless.

She leaned close to him like a Disney princess from another world and did some of those Marilyn things: tilted her head, hipped her hands, tossed her hair, squeezed her elbows forward, kissed the air between them, lowered her eyelids, and exhaled a long purrwhistling pucker kinds of things, then deftly flipped the pad and pencil out of the water with her big toe.

Did I mention that she was 10.2 feet tall?

And, she was the first woman he'd ever seen who seemed to relish her lower digits. She could've been the Sissy Hankshaw of footdom if she wasn't busy being a toe-boasting Marilyn Monroe amazon.

"Not yet," she whispered, pointing to a lone figure standing on a distant outcropping of ragged rocks.

Joltin' Joe.

Slugging something into the ocean.

It broke the surface like 2.2 flowers.

THE GREATEST RABBIT PUNCH

This is another true story, but I want to be clear: that's not the reason I'm including it. Not all true stories should be told. Some, in fact, should be snugged into a shoebox like a long-loved rabbit and buried in the back yard of childhood.

Oh, it's okay to place its last-nibbled carrot in there alongside it. It's okay to do it unceremoniously, alone. It's okay to even leave a marker that has temporary lawnmower immunity. But, a generation later, there should be nothing left for passers-by but a little depression in the ground where the shoebox collapsed.

This isn't one of those stories.

It happened at one of those rare moments in history, when all the airy tumblers of a single thunderclap fell into place, never to strike just that way, at just that place, ever again.

The world's then greatest boxer was once invited to receive an honorary degree from a college I was visiting. He was renowned for his singular skill in the art of formal human pummeling, but he'd also often demonstrated his virtuosity as an impromptu poet. That day was no exception:

"I like your school; I like your style, but I don't like your pay; I won't be back for a while," he'd said later at the press conference. Celebrated dead poets everywhere no doubt turned a little in their graves, but who cared about them. They were dead.

And, I'd like to see Carl Sandburg rope-a-dope with a stanza, dead or alive.

For my money, "Hog Butcher for the world" could never go the distance with "I can drown the drink of water, and kill a dead tree. Wait till you see Muhammad Ali."

I'll see your Chicago and raise you a lightning-fast jab, Carl.

That morning, my four-year old daughter was with me. I can't remember why, except that maybe it was my weekend to have her. Perhaps it was Liberal Arts Father-Visitor Daughter Day. Lucky for us, though, it was the same day the world's greatest rhyming boxer was to receive his publicity sheepskin.

Let's face it: giving an honorary college degree to a high-profile notable is a two-way street. Yes, the honoree is pleased to be post-secondarily validated without ever having to sit through an un-elective, but it also doesn't hurt the school's image.

Sometimes, the trustees later voted to stick up a statue near the athletic field. In my mind, I can't look at a statue without thinking about a favorite Vincent Price movie, but I might feel differently if it was me standing up there as a pigeon-shit depository. That's more than most of us ever achieve.

We arrived early, and I took her hand the best I could as she three-limb pinwheeled alongside me across a large open field to the reception house. To this day, I wish I'd pinwheeled along with her, but I was too distracted by the fear of having to return a daughter to a mother any less intact than how I'd received her.

I needn't have worried. Four-year olds are either indestructible or delicate as a feather, and she'd been delivered to me in full indestructible mode.

Today, I couldn't do a pinwheel if you stapled me to a windmill.

By the time we reached the reception house, she'd settled down into mere hop-a-long pull-toy mode, and I'd survived.

We went inside, and there, like a stop-motioned bolt of lightning, sat the man. The room was empty except for him, and he sat slumped on a couch, unmoving, staring at us. Impossible, but lightning is like that.

He immediately straightened up, smiled broadly and opened his arms toward us. Toward her.

"Hello, girl!" he said. I thought my daughter would do the natural thing, having never seen this big dark hulk of a man before, and immediately switch to snake mode around my leg.

Instead, she showed me how much fathers know about such things, and went right over to him in fearless kangaroo mode.

He picked her up and hugged her close as I stood across the room in abandoned lighthouse mode.

He opened his eyes wide in mock surprise and did the sitting version of a complementing pinwheel. She giggled and bobbled and matched him, twirl for playful twirl.

For my part, ships were going aground on the rocks over there by the dozens, and I couldn't move.

Soon, other people began entering the room. Statue-erectors and grown-up dead rabbit internors crowded in -- the usual

118

media blitz – and daughter and I were reduced to those subtle variations that you can never quite find in a picture puzzle.

I retrieved her from his arms like a reinstated lighthouse with a good excuse, no questions asked. When I moved in close to them, I saw that his face was bruised and swollen from a recent close fight. I was glad that she was still too caught up in child mode to notice this, or to know why if she had.

He returned her to me like a child alone placing a beloved pet in a shoebox.

Today, in her life's back yard, however, she still remembers and loves why the ground is shaped like that.

I hope he does, too.

B. Elwin Sherman is a humorist/author living in the New Hampshire North Country, where he writes a syndicated humor column and often reinvents "the cottage industry survival kit."

His books have gone largely unheralded, "because I do nothing to promote them. No one should ever have a legacy before they're dead. Life is embarrassing enough without that."

He first read Richard Gary Brautigan's works in college, "when everyone else was lugging around Nietzsche and Kant for ballast. I kept In Watermelon Sugar *in my hand because there was a tsunami on the horizon, and there I was without a beach umbrella."*

www.ingramcontent.com/pod-product-compliance
Lightning Source LLC
Chambersburg PA
CBHW031607260626
47154CB00020B/1699